Happy Princess

Additional Titles
by Stephanie Perry Moore

Preteen
Carmen Browne Series

Book 1   True Friends

Book 2   Sweet Honesty

Book 3   Golden Spirit

Book 4   Perfect Joy

Teen
Payton Skky Series

Book 1   Staying Pure

Book 2   Sober Faith

Book 3   Saved Race

Book 4   Sweetest Gift

Book 5   Surrendered Heart

Laurel Shadrach Series

Book 1   Purity Reigns

Book 2   Totally Free

Book 3   Equally Yoked

Book 4   Absolutely Worthy

Book 5   Finally Sure

5
Carmen Browne Series

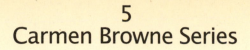

Happy Princess

Stephanie Perry Moore

MOODY PUBLISHERS
CHICAGO

All Scripture quotations are taken from the King James Version.

Editor: Tanya Harper
Cover Design: Jaxson Communications
Interior Design: Ragont Design3

ISBN-13: 978-0-8024-8171-9
Printed by Color House Graphics in Grand Rapids, MI – May 2013

Library of Congress Cataloging-in-Publication Data

Moore, Stephanie Perry.
  Happy princess / by Stephanie Perry Moore.
      p. cm.—(Carmen Browne series; bk. #5)
  Summary: Eleven-year-old Carmen finds with the help of God she can face
the new challenges of starting menstruation, and her relationships with her
girlfriends, family, and boys.
  ISBN-13: 978-0-8024-8171-9
  ISBN-10: 0-8024-8171-X
  [1. Friendship—Fiction. 2. Menstruation—Fiction. 3. Chris-tian life—
Fiction. 4. African Americans—Fiction. 5. Virginia—Fiction.] I. Title.

PZ7.M788125Hap 2007
[Fic]—dc22

2006028796

3 5 7 9 10 8 6 4

Printed in the United States of America

For
Elizabeth Wood
(my sweet middle school PE teacher and cheerleading coach)

I haven't forgotten that years ago they called me your twin.
Your excitement for life and concern
for people rubbed off on me.
Thanks for caring so much—
the extra you gave made a difference.
May each reader know they are
as special to the Lord as you made me feel!

Contents

Acknowledgments   9

1. High Spirits   11

2. I Believe   25

3. Played Out   37

4. Drama Queen   51

5. More Surprises   61

6. Not Rich   77

7. Truly Royal   87

8. Cloud Nine   97

9. Blissful Angel   107

Acknowledgments

Boy, am I happy and glad to be feeling great. See, last week I was down for ten days with a kidney infection. My husband and daughters were worried about me because I was in such intense pain. Thankfully, I was blessed to have my mom come up and take care of me and my family. Her positive presence nursed me back to health. Though medicine from the doctor was needed, her dose of love helped as well.

It reminded me of days gone by when I was her little girl. Honestly, there were many days that my cycle tried to get me down. However, my mom reminded me that dwelling on what hurts won't fix things. She taught me how rest was important and how to ask the Lord for comfort. I know having a changing body can bring on mixed feelings. Just remember you're a child of the King and He won't put more on you than you can bear. And look for your angels here on earth that can help you shine, like the people below help me.

To my parents, Dr. Franklin and Shirley Perry, Sr., thanks for giving me more than I needed. Looking back, I was treated like royalty. Happy to have you as parents.

To my publisher, Moody/Lift Every Voice, and especially the editor, Tanya Harper, I'm grateful. What a blessing to have done this sweet series with you. Happy you gave it a chance.

For my brother, Dennis Perry Jr., thanks for being there for your big sis. The precious memories we share growing up in the house together will forever connect us. Happy we're still close.

To my endearing princesses, Sydni and Sheldyn, thanks for giving your all in school. Everything in life won't be easy, but hard work pays off. Happy God gave you to me.

To my hubby, Coach Moore, thanks for all you do for our family. I love being your queen. Happy you are my heart.

To my wonderful readers, thanks for letting this series make a difference in your life. Know that you are worthy of greatness. Happy if this book makes you smile.

And to the King of Kings, thanks for giving me strength to finish another series. I'm so thankful for the creative gift You've given me. Happy to be a jewel in Your crown.

1

High Spirits

Christmas Eve day was shaping up to be so much fun. My mom and I had just finished shopping for our family and friends. She was dropping me off at the skating rink for a Christmas bash from three to five o'clock. My friends Riana, Layah, and Imani were all waiting for me by the front door. Of course, my mom lectured us about being careful, even though her friend Miss Pam, who was one of the owners, promised that she'd keep an eye on us. We also had strict instructions that when the DJ announced the last song, to start getting our stuff together right after that. That would be easy since all of us brought our own skates, and we wouldn't have to stand in long lines to turn in rented ones.

Mom rolled her window down to say hello to Miss Pam. "Hey, girl. Thanks for letting Carmen and her friends hang out today. They know how to behave and what's expected of them." Then my mom gave us a look. "Right, ladies?"

"Yesss," we all said together, anticipating jumping out of the car.

"Girl, you know I can handle things. Plus, I know that Carmen Browne and any friends of hers behave like such *ladies*," Miss Pam said, winking at us.

As soon as Mom pulled off, we darted inside to begin our party time. It wasn't that we planned to do anything wrong that would displease our parents; it's just that me and my girls couldn't wait to just hang out with each other. Before we put our skates on, we decided to exchange Christmas gifts.

Imani went first. She handed all of us a cute, small, square box. Inside was a wallet that turned into a purse, if you put on the long strap. They were in the cutest colors. I had a pink one. She gave Riana purple. Layah had orange, and then Imani pulled hers out. It was bright gold. I took my money out of my back pocket so fast and put it in my new gift.

We all said thank you, and she said, "Just a little somethin' I wanted to give you guys to carry, because you carried me these last few months when I was trippin'. It's great to have y'all as friends."

Then it was Layah's turn. She gave us airbrushed sweatshirts with our names on the back! They were *sooo* cute. We agreed to go to the bathroom and put them on as soon as we were done exchanging gifts.

"I thought it'd be fun to look alike," Layah said.

Riana handed us pretty gift bags from Bath & Body Works with fragrances inside. She gave us each the same one, Warm Vanilla Sugar. I loved splashing on my mom's sprays. Now I'd have my own. *But how will I keep my little sister Cassie out of mine?* I wondered. Smiling, I realized I could share.

"I thought it would be cool for all of us to wear the same fragrance," Riana said. "Now we can really be sweet."

My gift was last. I handed a small jewelry box to each of them. They didn't even notice the shiny new chain that I was wearing. It was an adorable necklace that said, "Best Friends Forever." They opened their boxes . . . and all three of them loved it.

"We're best friends for life," I said.

We ran to the bathroom to put on our sweatshirts and necklaces, giggling and discussing how excited we were to have each other as friends. Sometimes it was difficult dealing with different personalities. But nothing could break us up.

Just as quickly as I thought that, I saw my friend Spencer and Hunter enter the skating rink. Spence, as everyone called him, had a big smile on his face. He looked happy to see us, and it was cool seeing him. He came over and spoke to us. Then he asked me to skate a few times around with him. Sounded good to me. I gave my friends a quick wave good-bye, and I noticed little frowns on their faces, but I couldn't let them "steal my joy" as my grandma always said.

We skated around side by side. The DJ was really jammin'.

He went back to his buddy and I went back to my girls. When I skated toward Layah and Imani, they skated away. They waved at me and gave each other high fives. The nerve. I was glad I was past taking things personal. I came. They left. So what. No big deal.

Just then I saw Riana a second too late. Tripping, I ran into her, nearly knocking her down.

"Girl! Carmen, you almost made me drop my nachos," she said to me in an evil tone.

"It was an accident. I'm sorry. What's wrong with you, Riana? Please tell me you're not mad at me for skating with Spence."

"No, I'm cool with that. It's just. . . ."

"What?" I asked, hanging on for her next word.

"I wish Hunter would say something to me. He just waved and left."

"Did you say anything to him?"

"I shouldn't have to. Spence came over to you."

"Forget him. He's not the only boy in the world. Let him see you having a good time, girl. One thing having a big brother has taught me, and you should know this 'cause your brother's the same way; boys are a trip! This is girlfriend time now anyway. You ready?"

"Yeah, let's do this. You're right. If he doesn't wanna talk to me, I am not tryin' to chase him. Let's go."

It's funny how I told Riana that this was girlfriend time, but the first person I skated with when I got here was Spence, I thought to myself. *Maybe it was friend time.*

Riana and I skated right into Layah and Imani. This time Riana and I got our feet all tangled up together in the excitement. The four of us ended up on the hard floor. Immediately, everyone started cracking up . . . except Layah.

"Oww! Get off of me!" she said rudely. "Y'all need to watch where you're goin'!"

Layah and Imani skated away.

"What's her problem?" I said to Riana, hoping she knew what was up with Layah.

Layah was smiling one minute. Then the next she had an attitude.

Riana and I went to the concession stand to get something to drink, and Miss Pam asked if we were enjoying ourselves.

"Miss Pam, our friend Layah has an attitude, and our other friend Imani just skated off with her," I said.

"Well, I trust that you ladies can work it out," Miss Pam said, smiling.

"I hope so," I said, sighing.

Riana replied, "Let's go talk to them, Carmen."

I hoped Layah wasn't upset because of Spence. Why couldn't we stay cool? We had just made a pact to be friends for life, and now this. My older brother Clay said that girls always "keep somethin' goin.'"

When we didn't see Layah or Imani in the rink, we decided to check the bathroom. One of the many points in my mom's lecture before she dropped me off was, don't go to the bathroom alone. She said that at least two of us should always be together. Like a buddy system.

We opened the door and there they were. Imani had her arm around Layah, as Layah leaned against the wall holding her stomach. *She's probably faking,* I thought. "You know what? I'm not trying to be mean or anything. But I don't understand you. Why do you have to spoil everything? Everyone is trying to have a good time. You know we didn't mean to fall on you. What's up with you?"

Imani blurted out, "She started her period."

"What? Her period?" I asked, shocked.

Layah said, "I started my period! And I don't know . . . but I just feel weird . . . my stomach hurts! How would you feel if your cycle started at a skating rink?!"

"For real Layah? You started your period?" Riana asked, patting Layah on the shoulder.

"Yeah, Riana, I did."

Then Miss Pam walked in.

"Girls, is everything okay?" Miss Pam asked.

We all looked at each other, unsure of what to say.

"Umm . . . ", I muttered.

"Talk to me. What's going on?" Miss Pam questioned.

"Well, Layah just started—" Imani blurted.

"Imani, I can talk for myself. Miss Pam, my period started."

"Honey, was this your first one?"

"Yes," Layah replied.

"Were you already prepared with sanitary napkins?" Miss Pam asked.

"No, but my grandmother told me what to do if it hap-

16

pened to me in a public place. So I checked the sanitary napkin dispenser, and put my money in and got a napkin. My grandma said that if I couldn't get a napkin, then to just use toilet paper or paper towels until I could get what I needed," Layah said.

"Well, Layah, it sounds like your grandmother prepared you with information," Miss Pam said.

"You need to give your grandmother a call to let her know what's going on," Miss Pam said as we walked toward her office.

Even though I thought we had everything under control, I was glad that Miss Pam was there to help.

After Layah called her grandma we continued our celebration. I put aside being angry at her. Now I wanted to trade places with her.

"I can't wait for my cycle to start," I said. "I'm ready to be a woman."

"Me too," Riana chimed in.

"Me three," Imani said, being silly.

"Please. Y'all just don't know. Just wait. It's not all that."

All I could think about on the ride home was, *God, when is my time coming?*

★

Christmas morning I awakened to a busy household. Since I was getting older, the excitement of getting toys was gone, but I was hoping for a few outfits. I was excited to sleep in, or at least I thought that was the case, until Cassie woke me up. We shared her room while my grandparents were visiting.

"Carmen, you gotta come and see! You have a whole bunch of stuff under the tree. You better get up, girl."

My family and I said "Merry Christmas" to one another.

I thought Cassie had made a big deal out of nothing. But she wouldn't let me sleep. I saw a big box with "Carmen" on it. I had asked for a new computer . . . but it couldn't be. My dad told me I wasn't getting one of my *own* just yet. But I couldn't lift the heavy box with the angel wrapping.

"Go ahead and open it, sweetie," my dad said as my mom smiled.

I quickly tore the wrapping paper. And it was a computer! This had to be the best Christmas ever.

"Oh, thank you, thank you, thank you," I said, planting kisses on my parents.

"We're proud of how you've been working really hard to pull up your grades," Dad said. "I'll hook it up in your room later. But when it comes to surfing the Internet, Carmen, you'll still use the computer in the family room for that. *Understand*?"

"Oh, yes, Dad."

I opened the rest of my gifts, which included cute outfits, gospel CDs, and books. Christmas wasn't about getting, but it sure felt good to receive.

"Well, now that everyone has opened their gifts, I'm going to take about an hour or so in the studio, putting finishing touches on my project," Mom said.

I was glad to see her doing what she loved, because for a while she'd been undergoing all sorts of medical tests. Doctors had suspected that she might have breast cancer. It had been a difficult time for our entire family. I was so happy that my mom was healthy.

Later that afternoon I didn't know what to do with myself. So much was going on around my house. My brother and granddad were outside chopping logs. *Carmen Browne chopping logs? No way.* I could tell that they were bonding, so I didn't interrupt.

I went to the family room where my dad, who is head coach of the Virginia State football team, was hanging out with a few of his players. They stopped by to wish our family a Merry Christmas. Though I wanted everyone to be happy on this holiday, I wished I could just hang out with my dad. But I had to share him.

Coming from the kitchen was a delicious smell that seemed to call my name, so I headed there to see what was cooking. Cassie had an apron tied around her waist and was at the table busily stirring something in a bowl. That girl thought she could look just as cool as them. My grandmothers were busy chopping and slicing this and that. I asked if they needed another hand, but I was shooed away.

I knew my mom needed time for her project. *But didn't she say she'd be done in an hour?* I needed to check on her to see if she needed a sandwich, something to drink, an extra hand, whatever. I tapped on her door and walked in.

"Hey, Mom!"

Quickly she snapped, "Carmen, you can't just walk in, honey. You have to wait for me to say come in. I'm working, baby. What is it?"

"Sorry, Mom," I responded in a disappointed tone. "I just wanted to see if you needed anything."

"No, dear. I have everything I need. I'm trying to finish up this piece before dinner, okay?"

I didn't know why she had to bark at me. It was already past an hour. But I realized deep down she didn't mean to hurt my feelings.

Okay, Lord, I don't want to be in a sad mood. Help me out here. That's when I realized I could find joy just hanging out with myself. Over the past year, I had moved to a new city and had to make new friends. Then I had problems with those friends. I ended up on my own for most of the first semester of middle school anyway.

Since it was Christmas, I decided to read from the book of Luke about Jesus' birth. I didn't realize how much time had flown by until Mom came into my room. I had been reading and playing my Kierra Sheard gospel CD for a couple of hours.

"Let's set the table for dinner, sweetie. What are you reading?" she said, peering around the corner of my bedroom door.

"I was reading about the birth of Jesus. Trying to spend time with God. We do that to get to know Him better, right?"

"That's right, honey. Just like a new friend that you're getting to know. People can tell you about the person, but until you spend personal time with them, you don't really know them for yourself.

"I owe you a big apology. I'm sorry for being short with you like I did earlier."

"It's okay, Mom, I understand."

"I've been thinking that maybe it's time for you and I to *talk* some more."

"Talk more about what?" I asked, sort of confused.

"Well, sweetie . . . girl things. Menstruation. Cramps. You're at an age where you may be getting your cycle soon. I've tried to explain things to you in stages, when I've felt you were ready. And when you got home you told me one of your best friends just started her cycle yesterday at the skating rink."

"Mom, when did you say you started your cycle?"

"I was eleven, so there's a possibility that yours could begin in the near future. Some girls begin earlier than others. It just depends. Once you get your period, you'll have it for many years. That's the way God designed it."

"Do you still have yours?"

"Yep! And I'm nearly forty. That's why I'm apologizing, because sometimes your cycle can bring discomfort and irritability. I usually have a handle on it. But I let it get the best of me today. I allowed stress and fear of not meeting my deadline upset me. I should've budgeted my time better, so that I wouldn't be working on Christmas Day anyway. This is family time."

I hugged her. "Really, it's okay."

"Anyhow, we'll keep up with your cycle by charting it and marking the calendar, so you'll know pretty much when to expect it, and you'll be prepared."

"Like preparing for a big storm or hurricane?" I asked.

"Well, I don't want you to look at your cycle as being destructive like a hurricane, or to have a negative view of it. You'll probably hear some girls refer to it as a 'curse,' but it's not. It's the way that God designed the female reproductive system to function." My mom laughed and pinched my cheeks. "But you certainly do need to prepare and have the appropriate supplies.

"Several months before your cycle begins, you may notice a wet, clear substance in your underwear. That's called menarche. When your cycle actually begins, you may experience cramping at first, or see blood in your underwear, which might appear red or brown."

"Well, I'm just glad I have you. I feel bad 'cause Layah doesn't have her mother to talk to."

"But she has her grandma, honey. God is looking out for all you little ladies. I can't believe how you all are just growing up on us. I'm so glad that Miss Pam was there to help."

"Yeah, I was glad too, but I think we could've handled it."

"I know you all are at the age where you feel like you've got all the answers," she said, pinching my cheeks again.

"I love you, Mom."

"I love you back, Carmen."

We left my room arm in arm, on our way to set the

dinner table. If I trusted God with my life, He would work things out. I wasn't going to doubt Him. This Christmas wasn't so bad after all.

On Sunday morning both of my grandmothers were whipping up a huge Sunday morning breakfast as we prepared for church. Pancakes, French toast, sausage, Canadian bacon, eggs, hash browns, homemade biscuits, with coffee, tea, and orange and pineapple juice to drink. My grandmas *always* went overboard!

At church Pastor Wright spoke from Galatians 5:22–23 about the fruit of the Spirit. As Christians we're supposed to demonstrate love, joy, peace, long-suffering, kindness, goodness, faithfulness, gentleness, and self-control. *Me? Do all of that!?*

"Regardless of circumstances," Pastor Wright preached, "and of how we feel, we must obey God's Word. The Holy Spirit empowers us to live for Him. We can't exercise the fruit of the Spirit without that power. He should always be in control."

"Amen!" everyone shouted.

I concentrated on Pastor Wright's sermon. If I let God be in control of everything: how I relate to my parents, my siblings, and friends, I could have peace and not worry—even about my cycle, which my mom said might start soon. Silently I prayed, *Lord, help me to be patient and wait for You to make changes in my life. I know that sometimes I get anxious and want to grow up fast. Show me how to be an eleven-year-old who can have fun and still please You. In Jesus' name. Amen.*

I left church feeling good that day. The Holy Spirit gave me power to live. As we sang the benediction song, "Till We Meet Again," all the church was rocking. We were uplifting God with our *high spirits*.

2

I Believe

My family trailed my grandparents back to North Carolina. All of us, including my dad's parents, went to my mother's mom's house to celebrate the new year. Even Auntie Chris and Uncle Mark were there. It was good to see them, since we didn't spend time with them on Christmas.

I was so happy for Auntie Chris and Uncle Mark. My parents said that God had really helped them to work things out. Though I was only eleven, I knew that adults always fussing wasn't a good thing. Thankfully it looked like that chapter was behind them. I must admit, I still thought about how mean Uncle Mark was when Cassie and I last visited. However, I was trying to forget it and move on.

We sat around the den drinking hot chocolate with marshmallows. Mom said that we should talk about our plans for the new year.

Cassie jumped up and said, "I plan to be more like my sister. She's sweet, popular, and cool. And a lot of things that used to bother me about her don't bother me anymore."

I just smiled.

Then Clay took the floor. "I plan to do better with my studies. Not just academics, but letting Dad help me more with football fundamentals. I want to be able to execute difficult offensive schemes in high school. I need to be sharper. And I don't plan to be so stubborn."

Next my mom spoke up. "I'm going to balance my time better between work and my family. This last project just took a little bit more of my time than I wanted it to, and I will see to it that that doesn't happen again. Honey?" my mom said, signaling Dad that it was his turn.

"Next year professionally, God willing, I want to win the title that my team came up a game short of winning this year. And Mom and I will spend more time with our parents."

"That's right you should honor and treasure your elders," one of my grandmas said, laughing.

"Okay, I'm next," I said. "I just want to get along better with everyone. Last year there was so much drama. I just want to do better this year. I want to make my parents and God proud."

All of a sudden my aunt had a strange look on her face. She grabbed her stomach. Uncle Mark asked her if she was okay.

"Okay, Chris . . . honey, just be calm," Uncle Mark said nervously.

"I am, Mark. I felt a sharp pain, but let's just wait to see if I feel anything again before I call my doctor," Auntie Chris said. "I'm sure it's nothing."

My grandma said, "Chris, we've got so much baby birthin' experience in this room till you don't have to worry about nothin', honey."

Dad's mom said, "Child, you know that's the truth."

Mom, Dad, and Uncle Mark all started laughing.

We enjoyed the rest of our family time by playing board games and even performing an *American Idol*-like talent show. What a fun way to bring in the new year.

✪

Even though I enjoyed my Christmas vacation, I was excited to start school again. My grades had improved since last semester, and I was ready to start this one on the right track. Riana, Imani, Layah, and I walked through the hall together. We couldn't wait till fourth period because we'd finally have a class together. Health. Everybody knew health was an easy class, so the teacher would probably allow us to chat, once we finished our work. We needed to catch up on our girl talk.

"See you later, girlfriends!" Imani said to us.

"Smooches!" Riana said back.

"Y'all better go on to class with all that!" Layah said sarcastically.

I just cracked up at my friends acting silly.

When we broke up and went our separate ways to class, I was startled by someone who said "Boo!" right behind me. It was Spence.

"Heeey!" I said, pleased to see him.

"Carmen Browne, what's up?"

"I'm cool, Spence."

Realizing class would be starting soon, we looked at our class schedules and started putting a little pep in our step. We had first and sixth period together and started walking to our first period math class.

"How was your holiday, Spence?"

"Not too good."

"Why?"

"My dad came to visit. I live with my grandparents because my dad has had drug problems for a while. Now he says that he's not on drugs anymore. He wants me to come live with him, because he says he's gotten his life back together. That caused a lot of problems over the Christmas vacation. My grandparents are not sure if he's telling the truth."

"You might have to move away?" I asked, shocked.

Spence was the first boy who I thought was really cool. *And now he has to move?*

"You can't move away," I said.

"But my grandparents might not have a choice. They said we have to wait until the end of the school year to see."

"Do you believe that your dad's okay now?"

"I'm not sure. My grandparents are all I've ever really known. Yeah, they're older and stuff, but that's okay. Granddad does so much with me. Unfortunately, my dad's a stranger to me. I know that my grandparents are disappointed with their son. They said they didn't raise him to be like that."

I just sort of looked at Spence, not knowing what to say as we headed into math class. I felt really bad for him. It even made me think about my brother Clay and how he was adopted into our family. At my desk I prayed silently, *Lord, be with my friend. I hope his dad is really better. But since he wants to stay with his grandparents, would You make that happen? Maybe he could just visit his dad on the weekends or something. I know You can work it out. In Jesus' name. Amen.*

When class ended I tapped Spence's shoulder. "Spence, I hope everything works out. I'm praying for you."

He just smiled. I was so glad to learn to care about other people's problems.

The first day back to school was flying by so quickly. The teachers were merely going over the new curriculum. When it was lunchtime, I got to eat with my crew.

Imani said, "You guys know what health class is about, right?"

"Yeah, the permission slip that our parents signed said that we're talking about periods and stuff," I replied.

Riana said, "My brother told me that our teacher, Miss Wade, is mean. All that talking and stuff we thought we were going to be able to do? He told me that we could forget that."

As we put our trays up, gathered our stuff, and walked toward health class, the four of us were *not* excited. We didn't want a mean teacher, especially to talk to about our changing

bodies and other personal things. On top of Miss Wade being
mean, there was another surprise awaiting us when we
walked in her class. Our names were posted on the desks. Assigned seats! We weren't babies. In sixth grade, the teachers
let us choose our own seats, as long as our conduct didn't get
out of hand. Miss Wade lived up to her reputation.

"In this class you can't sit *just* anywhere," she said, order-
ing us around. "Find your name and have a seat. We have
work to do."

"All you had to do was tell us," Layah said under her
breath.

"Did someone say something smart?"

She had really good ears. She was not somebody to play
with. I hoped these fifty minutes would go fast like the morning time.

"Did everyone get their permission slips signed?" She
scanned the room as everyone nodded. "Okay, great. Pass
them forward. There's a special textbook on your desk. Open
it to page twenty-four. I'm going to go over a few key points
about menstruation, and then I'll take questions. With everyone's participation, we can have a great learning experience."

I sighed. Imani was frowning. Riana and Layah looked
bored like the rest of the girls in our class.

"Let me read the title . . . *Menstruation in Adolescent Girls*.
Menstruation *usually* starts around the ages of twelve or thir-
teen, but it could start as early as age seven. Some girls might
begin as late as age sixteen."

"I wish that was me," Layah blurted out.

Sixteen? Lord, that's when I'll start driving. My mind was racing a million miles an hour.

"Hold your comments until it's time," Miss Wade said.

Miss Wade said that the beginning of a girl's cycle is called the menarche. "Ladies, you might notice a wet and clear substance in your underwear up to six months before your cycle begins."

"I never heard that word 'menarche,'" some girl yelled.

"Okay, ladies, no more outbursts. I'll take comments and questions later. A menstrual period, cycle, or whichever term you choose, is a part of the female reproductive system. Every month the female body builds up a lining in the uterus. When the body determines that the lining is not needed, then it automatically sheds it. That shedding of blood is your period. Your period might come between every 22 to 35 days. When your cycle actually begins it may appear brown or red. This may vary from person to person. The first period is usually not a heavy one. It may be just a few drops of blood. So just because your period doesn't begin like your friend's, don't be alarmed. Everyone is different. Some of you girls might not have regular periods, especially in the beginning, and for some it may be there every month from the time that you start. Either way is normal. Everyone's body needs to take awhile to establish their regular menstrual cycle. And, girls, this is why you need to use a calendar to keep track of it. Some people refer to that process as *charting*."

She told us that menstruation might be accompanied by several symptoms. Cramps in the lower abdomen. Bloating in the tummy. Tender breasts. Headaches. Being tired. Mood swings and food cravings.

"Now the floor is open for questions and comments, ladies."

We sat there looking at each other.

"Ask me something, ladies . . . anything."

Nobody wanted to ask questions. My mom had explained everything to me. But I figured I'd ask questions for a girl who might've been afraid to ask. So I slowly raised my hand. I glanced at my friends. I'm sure they were wondering what I would say.

"Yes, Miss Browne, your question."

"Miss Wade, what did you say again about shedding a lining?"

"I'm glad that you want me to clarify that. During a menstrual cycle your body rids itself or sheds a lining in the uterus that is not needed. It's a very natural occurrence."

Another girl asked, "Am I going to have a period the rest of my life?"

"No, a woman's cycle usually ends between the ages of forty-five to fifty-five. Again, that varies from woman to woman."

"How long does a period last?" Imani asked.

"Generally between 3 to 7 days."

"Okay, I have a comment," Layah said raising her hand.

"Go ahead."

"Girls don't have to stop playing sports. We can even swim while we're on our periods," Layah said confidently.

Miss Wade said, "That's exactly right, Layah. You can do everything normally. You just need to make sure that you have a sanitary pad that is comfortable for you. You can find them at any grocery or drug store. If you happen to be near a public bathroom, most of them have machines that dispense individual pads. I brought a few samples for you all to see."

Everyone turned toward the table beside Miss Wade's desk. It was hard to imagine actually wearing a pad.

"What can I do to help my cramps?" a classmate asked.

"A number of things. You can exercise. Avoid extremely cold foods like ice cream. Salt and caffeine aren't good either. Hot tea works for some people. There's over-the-counter pain medication as well. Sometimes just lying down can help. If you have any more questions, I'm sure your parents or guardians would be interested in you talking with them about this."

With that comment, Miss Wade brought the question-and-answer session to a close. We were done for the day. The class actually turned out to be a very interesting one. Everyone became more comfortable the more we talked. Miss Wade wasn't so bad after all.

★

Two weeks later, my girls and I went to Imani's house for a sleepover. My mom hung around and talked to Imani's mom for a while. Riana's mom did too. Those three ladies had their own little party. Riana and I were happy when our moms left so the *real* party could begin. I said good-bye to my mom with a big hug and a kiss.

Imani's mom ordered pepperoni pizza, sausage pizza, buffalo wings, and nachos. We were ready to feast and watch a good movie.

Imani flipped the channel to a movie that I knew I wasn't supposed to be watching, but I felt weird and didn't want to say anything at first. I didn't want to seem like the "little baby" and ask Imani to turn. I just sat there squirming, listening to bad language. Finally, I spoke up.

"Imani, can you change the channel? I can't watch stuff like this."

"Yeah, right, *baby*. You're not at home. That's the *purpose* of a sleepover. Here you can do things that you can't do at home."

"Ummm. I don't agree with that, girl. We've been there and done that, before Riana and Carmen and I even knew you, and it got us in a whole lot of trouble," Layah said defiantly.

"Yeah, Imani, turn. We shouldn't be watching it," Riana chimed in.

"Uh, then y'all shoulda stayed at home. Over here we watch what I want to see," Imani said, looking at me eye-to-eye. "It's my house."

I got up.

"Where are you going?" Imani demanded to know from me.

"Don't worry, I'm not going to tell your mom what you're

doing. I'm going to call my mom and ask her to come and get me. You can get in trouble by yourself."

Layah and Riana got up and followed me.

"Now, all y'all want to leave like that? Fine then."

Before we could leave the room, Imani stood in front of me. "Okay, okay, okay. It's just that we don't have to always look at baby stuff. I didn't mean to make anybody uncomfortable."

The four of us did a group hug.

I was proud of myself. In health class I spoke up for any girls who may have been afraid to ask questions, and at Imani's sleepover, I took a stand because it was wrong to watch inappropriate movies. It's good to stand up for what's right. That's what *I believe*.

3

Played Out

When I woke up the next morning, I was shivering. I looked around me, and for a second I forgot where I was. Layah was a few inches away from me, with all the covers kicked off of her. I saw Imani hanging out of her bed. She had a smile plastered on her face. I didn't know what she was dreaming about, but she sure looked happy. When I rolled over to my left side, there was Riana, drooling on the pillow. Then I remembered. I was at the sleepover.

I couldn't go back to sleep. I looked up at the ceiling and pondered a few things. It was time the Lord and I had another serious chat. Silently I prayed, *Lord, last night started off pretty rough. It seems like my friends and I always find something to bicker about. But last night I had to take a stand. It wasn't right for us to watch a movie with bad language. Thank You for giving me courage. In Jesus' name. Amen.*

About an hour later, my mom came to pick me up. I waved bye to my friends. I was a little mad so I slammed the car door hard.

Even though I thanked God for giving me courage to stand up to Imani, I thought about what she said, and deep down I was tired of watching baby stuff too. I thought I could handle tougher things.

"Young lady, what's wrong with you? Just because you're getting picked up first. I don't even want to see that look."

I really didn't feel like talking to Mom about what happened. She was easy to talk to, but I just wasn't feelin' it. This time she had me figured out all wrong. I just shook my head.

"That's not what's wrong with me," I said under my breath.

"What did you say, Carmen? What's goin' on? Your brother and sister are the same way sometimes. You guys can be so unappreciative."

"No, no, I don't mind having to leave," I responded in an uptight voice.

"Well, what's wrong, then? Your face is looking as sad and pitiful as this dreary day."

"I'm sorry, Mom. It's nothing."

"It's something . . . but okay. You know I'm here when you're ready to talk."

We drove the rest of the way home in silence. My mom

was playing a Fred Hammond CD. The words said that your
every step was ordered if you were a righteous person. I
could hear my parents' voices in my head saying, "Carmen,
you'll grow up soon enough, and when you do, you still need
to be careful of what you watch." *I know, I know*, I thought to
myself.

★

In health class the next week, I aced the test. However,
none of that knowledge would help bring my cycle on any
sooner.

Riana and Layah walked to their next class, while Imani
and I headed the opposite direction to our PE class.

Imani asked me, "Carmen, what's wrong with you?"

"Nothing," I said, really dry.

"You sure?"

"Imani, I don't know. It's just that I feel like a little kid.
I'm tired of waiting for stuff to happen for me. Layah has her
cycle and I just want mine to start."

"I don't have mine yet. Riana hasn't started either," Imani
said.

"Yeah, but even though we're all the same age in number,
I'm six months older than Layah, and four months older than
you and Riana."

"Girl, you know that age doesn't matter. I wish mine
would start too. Anyway, we better get to gym."

At least I wasn't by myself.

★

Later when I got home from school, my mom told me to pick up the phone.

"Hello," I said, placing my book bag down.

"Hey, Carmen. How's my gingersnap doing?"

"Auntie Chris!" I said, finally excited about something. "I've been thinking about you. Mom said you were doing good."

"Yep. I had to call my favorite people. What's going on with my little girl?"

"That's just it. I don't want to be a little girl."

"What?"

"Auntie, I want to grow up."

"You *are* growing up, Carmen."

"My friend Layah has her cycle, and I'm older than she is! I know you're going to tell me that age doesn't matter."

"You're right. You said it yourself! Well, I'm glad I called because I know how it feels to want something your friends have. All my girlfriends in college had children before me. I didn't know why it was taking me so long. But I learned that God knows best. I had stuff in my marriage to work out. His timing was just right for me, and I know it will be perfect for you too."

I was listening to what my auntie was saying. She was making a lot of sense for her situation, but my situation seemed different to me.

"I hear you quiet over there. Not saying a word. No

amens or nothin'. The point is, Carmen, you just went through a whole episode of jealousy and envy with your friends."

"I know, but it's not that! I don't wish that Layah didn't have hers. I just want to have one too."

"Honey, that's the same thing. Were you excited for her experiencing something new?"

I was thinking about how Layah actually complained a lot about her cycle. But I didn't want to say that to my auntie, because she'd probably say, *See, I told you not to want to be like someone else.*

"Your time will come, Carmen. Also, I just want to be real with you. Sometimes it seems like I've had my cycle forever. Trust me when I say, you'd better enjoy these days. And if your friend Layah was honest, she's probably had days when she wished she didn't have it because of cramps or irritability or whatever."

How did she know? I thought smiling.

Talking to her made me feel better. I wasn't going to be mad about what I didn't have anymore.

"Thanks, Auntie Chris. I love you."

"Love you too, Carmen."

"Say hi to Uncle Mark."

"Okay, I will, honey. Bye."

"Bye, Auntie."

✦

It was Valentine's Day. Dad always made sure that his "sugar lumps"—Mom, Cassie, and me—had the most beautiful cards and delicious chocolates. Mom loved truffles, Cassie liked chocolate covered peanuts, and I just had to have juicy chocolate-covered strawberries. Clay wasn't left out. He always asked for a triple cheeseburger or something like that.

Everybody at school was all abuzz about who would be getting cards and all that. Kids passed out cards in elementary school, but this was different. In middle school, you got cool points if there was someone who liked you.

As I walked to class, Spence came up to me and handed me a card with a heart-shaped sucker and a cute little bear on the card. The card said, "I Like You Beary Much!" That was so sweet. Spence said that he had a dental appointment, so he would only be in school for a half day; we wouldn't see each other at lunchtime.

I checked my locker for a binder and some extra pens; then I saw Imani walk past.

I couldn't wait to tell someone about my card. She could be a good listener sometimes.

"Hey, girl!" I shouted. "Let's walk to class together."

"Carmen, I'll have to catch up with you later!" Imani said, giving me the quick brush-off.

I wondered where she was going so fast. We still had five minutes before the bell would ring. I couldn't wait until I saw her again to find out why she left so quickly.

At lunchtime Riana, Layah, Imani, and I were eating at our usual table. I showed them the card that Spence gave me. They thought it was so cute. The three of us were laughing and joking, but I was not talking to Imani. Every time Imani tried to start a conversation with me, I couldn't get out of my mind how she wouldn't even give me a minute of her time. So I figured if she wanted to talk to me, then we would see about *that*.

"Imani, why did you dis me earlier in the hallway?" I questioned, shocking her.

She looked at me as if I was saying something that wasn't true. I looked back at her the same way, waiting for her answer.

"First of all, I didn't dis you."

"Well, what do you call it?" I asked impatiently.

"Carmen, I needed to talk to my teacher before class. And I didn't feel like hearing you go on and on about Spence. You're sweatin' over nothin'. I'll see you guys in health," Imani said as she got up from the table. "My appetite is spoiled."

"You don't even know what I was gonna say, Imani." *She was right, though.*

Giving me a look like "yeah, right," Imani stormed off from our table.

"Carmen, you upset her," Riana said.

"I don't care about her being upset."

"Hey, don't get mad at me," Riana said, eating her last bite of Jell-O.

As we left the cafeteria and walked to class, Layah asked if we were going to the basketball game tomorrow after school. Riana said yes. I hadn't even asked my parents yet.

"Girl, everybody is going to be there. You should come," Layah said.

Because my grades had improved and Clay was going, I was pretty sure that I could go.

The gym was so crowded. It was like the whole school came. We were playing our county rivals, Salem Middle School. Layah told me that Imani would look for us. I really didn't know if I *wanted* her to.

Riana said, "I don't know how Imani's going to find us in this crowded gym."

I pretended like I didn't hear her. "We need to make sure we stick close together 'cause my mom's picking us up," I reminded Layah and Riana.

That was the good thing about my mom finishing up a project. She had a little downtime, and she was there for me and my friends. She was happy to pick us up from the game.

"Is Imani riding home with us?" Riana asked me as we found a seat twelve rows behind our team.

"I hope not," I said, rolling my eyes.

Riana said, "Ohh . . . I won't mention her name around *you* again. But you should cut her slack. She misses her dad and today is his birthday."

I felt awful. Imani never told me why her father didn't live with them, but I could only imagine not having a dad around could be hard.

The second quarter began. Layah and Riana scanned the bleachers to see if they could spot Imani. *They* didn't want her to sit alone.

I started to think about my stubborn attitude.

Growing up meant not taking things personally. I needed God to help me be a better friend.

Lord, my attitude has not been good toward Imani. She's supposed to be my friend, and she wasn't being very friendly earlier today. Also, now I know why I remember in Pastor Wright's sermon, when he said the Holy Spirit empowers us to exercise the fruit of the Spirit. That the Holy Spirit helps us to love and be patient with one another. My fruit was pretty rotten, huh? Thank You for another chance to do better. In Jesus' name. Amen.

★

National Signing Day for college football was coming up tomorrow, so my dad had been working very hard the last few weeks. He was on the road traveling, trying to recruit players, so we didn't really get to see much of him. I was so surprised that he wanted to spend daddy-daughter time together. He said that he wanted to spend individual time with Clay, Cassie, and me. But today was *my* day with daddy. We told corny knock-knock jokes, ate tacos, and just hung out.

Forget Spence. I had someone to care about me so much, and he would never let me down. Sitting under my dad's arm was peaceful and cozy. Then the phone rang. My dad answered it. I thought it would be a short call, but it was his offensive coordinator, Coach Dotson, and from the expression on his face, something was wrong. He got up from the sofa and hurried into his office; then his voice became louder.

"Are you serious? Those boys know better than that! In jail. Caught with drugs. Thanks, brother. I'll talk to you later when I figure out what to do about this."

"Honey!" he yelled to my mom after he hung up the phone.

"Just a minute, I'll be right there," Mom called out.

Dad came back and sat next to me.

"Sweetie, I'm sorry. I know we were having *our* time, but some of my players have gotten themselves in trouble."

"I heard you say drugs, Daddy."

"Yeah, I was talking so loud. I'm sorry, sweetie. They called Coach Dotson to bail them out, and then he called me. He really didn't want to call me because he knew I would be upset. And I *am*. Those boys know better. Just like Mom and I always tell you kids, we're raising you according to God's Word, and we expect certain things from you. When you do things that you shouldn't, the consequences can be severe. Do you understand?"

"Yes sir. I don't want to destroy my body with drugs, alcohol, or anything else."

My dad was just as serious about being a coach, as he was about being a parent. He always said that parenting was a lot like coaching, because in both roles his responsibility was to teach, train, and encourage.

Mom came into the family room, and he filled her in on what was going on. She just shook her head.

"Are those the same three who got into trouble at that dance, Charles?"

I felt really bad. He was hoping to get some of the state's top players. It was sad to see that they weren't coming to Virginia State.

"Well, you signed *some* players, right?"

"Yeah, but they're a different caliber or talent level . . . it's hard to explain, sweetie."

"No, I get it. Something you wanted didn't go the way you planned. It hurts. Trust me, Dad. I understand."

"As believers we have to continue to seek God's direction, and follow His leading for the next move that we should make. That can seem tougher when things are not going the way we want. But I've been on this earth a long time, and God takes care of everything, as long as we live His way and keep Him first. You just caught me having a moment, Carmen. Here I was trying to figure out what was next, but sitting here talking to my own daughter has encouraged me. I'll just trust God for the answers." Dad felt better about his problem. I had actually helped him see that he wasn't *played out*.

"Yep. The same knuckleheads. They don't learn. Or should I say they choose disobedience? The university certainly doesn't need any negative press, especially the day before signing. Parents who hear about this might be reluctant for their sons to play on a team with these issues."

"Honey, folks know you've worked hard to build such a good program. It's going to be okay. They know what a good coach you are, and that you can't be around your players 24-7."

"Well, I'm just kicking myself. I thought I taught them better than that."

"Charles, you did teach them better than that, and more importantly their parents probably did also. Some kids are going to make certain choices no matter what, but the important thing is that they've been caught. Unfortunately, sometimes they've got to learn the hard way."

"If it's not one thing, it's another with this team. I'm so glad I have you to keep me calm. I love you, babe. I'll be back later." My dad said, hugging Mom. "Come here, big girl," my dad said, reaching over to hug me.

It was weird. I hated my dad calling me that, and of course, I didn't want to upset him more, so I didn't say anything.

"You're a great coach, Dad."

"Thanks, honey."

✪

The next day at school, everybody came up to me and said that they saw my dad on TV, escorting his players from jail. In first period, some guys teased me.

"I heard your dad's tryin' to get some really big recruits, but he can't keep a handle on his team."

"Man leave her alone," Spence cut in.

"What you gon' do about it? Your granddad's the president. He should've gotten a tougher coach," a hefty boy named Travis said.

"If you knew anything about football, you'd know that Carmen's dad turned the program around. He's a great coach with *sixty* players on the team. *Three* players did something wrong. Not the whole team. They made their own choices. My granddad is probably going to extend Coach Brown's contract," Spence announced. "It's not like you could do any better."

"Yeah. Whatever," Travis shot back.

Travis and the other guy turned around in their seats as class was starting.

"Thanks, Spence. That was cool for you to look out for me like that."

❂

When I got home I was so surprised to see my dad's car in the driveway. I rushed inside and found him at the kitchen table looking like he was deep in thought.

"Dad? Are you okay?"

"Yeah, baby girl, it's been rough today. Come give me a hug."

Hugging him, I asked, "Where's Mom?"

"She had a doctor's appointment."

"She's all right?" I asked, hoping the doctor hadn't found something wrong.

"Yeah, she's fine. Just a routine checkup."

"Okay. That's good. But why do you look so sad? Let's talk."

"How's everything with you?" my dad asked.

But I didn't want to talk about me.

"Dad, let me make you a sandwich."

He smiled.

We ate peanut butter sandwiches.

"Mmm, that was delicious," he said, smiling.

"So Dad, what's going on with your players who got in trouble? Kids were talking about it today at school. Are things any better?"

"Well, Carmen, they've been suspended from the team and ordered to undergo counseling by the university. Because this is their second offense, they may be kicked out of school. We'll have to wait and see. Because of the actions of a few, several recruits that I thought were going to sign with me today backed out. Their parents sent them to other schools. But God will send more players. Talented ones too. The blessing in this whole mess is that my team really has a sense of how each person's *individual* behavior can reflect on a *whole* group."

4

Drama Queen

Valentine's Day wasn't the only important thing about February. The biggest thing to me was that my dad had always treated our family extra special on that day. However, as I sat in social studies class, my teacher, Miss Harry, emphasized the importance of Black History Month.

My school was predominantly African-American students and teachers. This month was a huge deal here. Black history facts were posted everywhere around the school, even at the water fountains. At the end of the month, we had a Black History Challenge. It was like a game show. The whole school would gather for an assembly and watch contestants answer questions. The top three students won $100 savings bonds. That made people want to study extra hard. Clay placed second in the contest.

Miss Harry was one of the few white teachers in the school. She was young, hip, cute, and very easy to relate to. She was also pretty funny.

Miss Harry said, "This morning we're going to talk about some important accomplishments by people of color. Many of those accomplishments brought great change to our society. But before we get into what the textbook says, I want to hear from you guys. Does anyone want to share any personal thoughts about black history this month?"

No one said a word. Then all of a sudden Hunter, Spence's friend and Haven and Hayli's brother, spoke up. He was always very quiet. Riana wanted to have a class with him, but they only passed one another in the hallway or at lunch. I was shocked when he spoke up in class. *Boy, if Riana could trade places with me now!*

"Well, basically African people came to America as slaves. They were abused and made to work for whites for so long. There were mean, hateful groups such as the Ku Klux Klan and outrageous laws, which kept the slaves from rising up and doing better for themselves. As time moved on and people changed, President Abraham Lincoln signed the Emancipation Proclamation, which freed slaves. Even though that was a long time ago, it took another big movement to bring more change, and that's when Martin Luther King Jr. came into the picture. My dad said, that's when black people stood together."

"Well, Hunter, I'm extremely impressed," Miss Harry said, clapping with us as we cheered him on.

Hunter was so silly. He stood up and took a bow. I was impressed too. What a great summary.

I couldn't imagine not being able to go to school and learn like white children. And pickin' cotton all day would be awful. There's no way I could stand seeing my father get whipped to death because he disagreed with some master. God is the only Master that anyone should have to obey and serve. Even the Lord gives us choices. After taking a moment and reflecting on the past, I was thankful I wasn't alive back then to experience it. I thought of it in a way that I never had before.

I raised my hand. "Miss Harry?"

"Yes, Carmen, you have something you want to contribute?"

"Yes, this is just a lot. I just think about a fountain that I couldn't drink from. Not being able to try on shoes at a department store. I flip through this textbook, and it's hard to imagine being treated so cruelly."

"I understand, honey," Miss Harry said.

People had to go through all that pain. That made me feel something. They went through a lot, so that today I could live better. I mean, I wasn't royalty or anything (Grandma always said we were a royal priesthood), but I wasn't a slave either. *What about the little black girl who lived two hundred years before me? The one who was a slave and had to watch as the little white girl got everything and she got nothing.*

It just didn't seem fair. It just didn't seem right. It was my history. Understanding it, embracing it, and claiming it made me stronger. *Hmm . . . maybe I'm maturing*, I thought.

❂

Over the next several days, I researched the Internet and encyclopedias and found so many African-Americans who made a difference. However, some names just kept popping up over and over again. Dr. Martin Luther King Jr., Reverend Jesse Jackson, Medgar Evers, Booker T. Washington, Frederick Douglas, Sojourner Truth, Madame C. J. Walker, Alex Haley, Andrew Young, Condoleeza Rice, Dr. Ben Carson, and many others.

One evening flipping through channels, I saw a preview of the miniseries *Roots*. It was coming on later that evening. I asked my parents if I could watch it. Actually, they thought that it would be good for us to watch as a family. All of us kids had so many questions. It was not easy to watch. If I didn't get it when Hunter broke it down to us in class, I sure got it by watching this series based on the family of author Alex Haley. His name came up during my Internet search. He told his ancestors' story from research and oral history passed down through his family.

"Kunta Kinte and his family had a hard life. Thanks to their sacrifices we can live better," Dad said.

"And if I could see them now, Dad, I would thank them all," I said.

"Kids, try to live your lives in such a way that if your ancestors *could* see it, they would be proud. Don't waste your time. They couldn't go to school. You can. You can pursue your dreams in a way that was nearly impossible for them. Don't stop believing you can achieve greatness. Ultimately if you live a live pleasing to God, that will honor them."

"Yep. That's what Rosa Parks did," Cassie said.

Cassie told us about the lady she admired in the civil rights movement. She was so tired one day and decided that "enough was enough," and refused to give up her seat to a white man. It didn't matter that she was breaking the segregation laws in Montgomery, Alabama, in 1955. She wasn't going to sit at the back of the bus. Mrs. Parks bravely sat in the front. Her bold actions sparked the civil rights movement.

I heard what Dad said, and I planned to follow his directions. I was determined to make the most of my life for myself and for others. And more importantly, for God who created me.

❂

The next day when I came home from school, Cassie was waiting for me in my bedroom. I was so tired, and the last thing I wanted to hear was Cassie whining about something. Instead of staying in my room, I placed my book bag by my bed and immediately did a one-hundred-and-eighty-degree turn, and headed back out for some privacy.

"No! Please don't go," Cassie said, grabbing my arm. "I'm

serious, Carmen. This is a big deal. I need a big sister to talk to. Please."

I'd never seen my sister act so seriously like she really, really needed me. *And then calling me big sister, wow. Something is definitely wrong*, I thought. I took my hand and felt her forehead and then her cheeks.

"Are you okay?" I said with a smile.

"This isn't a joke. I had the worst day of my life today at school!"

Cassie was only in fourth grade. *What could be so horrible?* She didn't know anything about problems. I was the big middle-schooler with all the drama. But I couldn't make light of it anymore. I'd hear her out. I sat down on my bed beside her.

"Okay. Tell me. What happened today?"

"Rolanda and I have been so cool."

I was hoping she would tell me something I didn't know. Besides, I knew she and Rolanda, Riana's little sister, were tight. *They couldn't possibly have problems,* I thought.

"Yeah, I know."

"You might think Rolanda is sweet, because every time she comes over she acts so nice and everything."

Riana had told me stories about her.

"Cassie, I've heard stories about how she can be mean sometimes from her sister."

"Okay, what I'm about to tell you, it won't be hard for you to believe then." She let out a sigh of relief.

"Just tell me, okay?"

"This year a new girl came to our class. Dee Dee. And she's really cool, Carmen. I gave her a bracelet, and Rolanda told her that she thought it was ugly."

"So what did Dee Dee say?"

"She said she thought it was too. She called the Valentine's gift that I gave her ugly, in front of everyone in our class. Everybody laughed. I was so embarrassed."

"Why do you think that Rolanda said the bracelet was ugly?"

"I think she was upset 'cause I didn't get her anything for Valentine's Day. But I gave Rolanda stuff for Christmas and I didn't get Dee Dee anything, so I figured I could give Dee Dee something for this holiday. And I don't know what to do, because I'm afraid that they don't want to be my friends anymore. Some days Rolanda tells me not to be Dee Dee's friend, and I just ignore her. But it seems like when Rolanda tells other people not to be my friend, they listen. Then I'm left out. I just wanna be popular like you."

"Cassie, you can try talking to Rolanda and Dee Dee, and telling them that you're upset. If they act like they don't care, then just ignore them. You can't make people be your friends. I bet if you ignore them, they'll try to be your friends again, but this time for *real*." Patting my sister on the back, I said, "As far as being popular, you just have to be yourself. And you have to pray. Ask God to help you see who your real friends are, and keep being a sweet person."

"Carmen, you're always so happy. You and your friends get along."

"Yeah, right," I said sarcastically. "We argue but we're still friends. They tell me when I hurt their feelings, and I tell them when they hurt mine."

"Thanks, Carmen. I knew talking to you would make me feel better. I'm going to try everything you said."

We gave each other a high five and she left my room. Right before dinner, I went to see what my brother was up to, and I found him sitting on his bed pouting.

"What's wrong with you?" I asked.

Clay just looked at me, as if to say why did I have to be nosy and get in his business.

"I got girl drama."

"Uh, oh. Well, let me leave you alone." I turned to exit.

"No, stay!" He motioned for me to walk in his direction. "Carmen, come in!"

"You want me to come in and talk to you about your girl problems?" I was shocked.

Something weird was going on here. Cassie wanted to talk. Then Clay thought I could help him. *Is God using me?*

"Are you feelin' okay, wantin' my help?" I placed my hand on his forehead just like I did to Cassie.

"Ha, ha, ha."

"So what's up?"

"You're a girl and I need your opinion. It's these sisters. I think you know them. Their brother is a sixth grader."

"The twins Hayli and Haven?"

"Yeah. Yeah. I told you. You know 'em."

I had overheard some girls while I was standing in the

lunch line, talking about the twins liking Clay.

"You're the one that both of them like?" I blurted out.

"How'd you know?" Clay said, not denying it.

"I have my sources," I said sarcastically.

"What are you gonna do? They're sisters."

"Carmen, I don't know. That's why I called you in here!"

"You need to be open with them."

"Well, that's the thing. I like one more than the other one. The one that I *don't* like—I never made her think that I liked her. I mean one time I did, but that's because I thought she was her sister. I get them mixed up sometimes until I start talking to them for a while. One of them is girlier than you are. She's so into clothes and nails and stuff. There's no way in the world that I could like her. The one that I like doesn't want her sister to be sad, so I don't think we'll ever talk or anything. I don't know."

"Just explain to them what happened with you mixing them up, and if they can work it out, then maybe you'll have a shot with the one you like."

"You think so?"

"It's worth a try. Be honest and they'll hear you out."

"Thanks, sis." My brother said, giving me the thumbs-up. "Sometimes, Carmen, you're not such a *drama queen*."

5

More Surprises

The next morning at breakfast, I was the last one downstairs to eat. I couldn't find one of my favorite shirts that I wanted to wear.

"I have something for you. Even though I already treated you for Valentine's Day, you are my sweetheart twelve months of the year! I have the best family in the world. You all have been so understanding with my hectic recruiting schedule. We're still trying to sign players who didn't commit anywhere else, so keep praying for our coaching staff."

"I will, Dad. Thanks for the gift. I understand you're busy," I said, opening up the velvet box.

It was such a pretty necklace and bracelet set. In cursive were the words "Daddy's Girl."

There was a pink diamond dotting the *i* in the word *girl*.

"I know you're growing up, Carmen," he said, reaching over to kiss me, "but you're always going to be my *little girl*. I can tell by the look on your face that you don't like for me to call you a little girl, but I just want you to know that you'll always have your daddy who loves you sincerely. Okay?"

"Aww, Daddy. I know. And this gift is off the chain! Oh, it's gonna look so good on me," I said as I ran over to my mom to put the necklace on me.

You would've thought it cost a million dollars or something, the way I was acting. I clutched it tight because it meant a lot to me.

"Now don't go trying to be all flashy at school today," my mom said. "You can wear it, but don't show off in front of your friends. People see even a small diamond and lose their minds, okay?"

"Yes, ma'am, I won't brag." I said, hugging my mom.

Cassie and Clay had finished breakfast and were in the family room checking their backpacks.

My dad gave Cassie earrings and a ring that said "Daddy's Heart." Clay got a watch that said "Always time for you."

Cassie asked Dad, "What did you get Mommy?"

Mom held her hand out and showed us a ruby surrounded by sparkling diamonds.

"Wow! You're blingin' Mom," Cassie said, examining my mom's hand.

"Yeah, Mom, that's a sweet ring," I said.

"Dad hooked you up, Mom," Clay said, laughing.

Not only did my mom get a ring, but Dad planned to take her on a cruise too, since their anniversary was in February. They were going to Ocho Rios, Jamaica. They showed us pictures of the resort, off the coast of pretty blue water.

My grandmother was coming to town to take care of us. We couldn't go because we were in school, and my parents needed to have their special time together. They promised that the entire family would go somewhere special this summer.

I had mixed feelings about my grandma keeping us. She could be so fussy. She liked things extra neat. I didn't wanna clean all the time. The good part was that she was staying in our parents' room. That meant I didn't have to share my room with Cassie.

Before my parents left, they sat the three of us down for a "talk." Dad said, "Okay, guys, you all know what we expect from you. Be respectful and on your best behavior. Your mom and I will be back in no time. Please don't call us about arguments or silly things. The last thing we need on our vacation is Grandma telling us how you guys 'showed out' while we were gone. Understand?"

We all said yes. We'd make our parents proud of us. I hoped anyway.

✪

"What do you all want for dinner?" my grandma asked later that night when she was in charge.

on my underwear. "And I have a headache."

"Well, your mama told me that you and her had just talked about this, and it looks like this is it. Sometimes it starts off brown in color, and sometimes later it'll show up red. I'm just glad you were here at home with me and not at school, baby. You know what I mean? Come here and give your grandma some suga'. It's your period!"

She squeezed me really tight. I was stunned. But it made sense. I remembered that Mom told me that it could start off brown! In health class, I learned the same thing.

"Mom keeps pads under this cabinet," I said, reaching for the package.

"You take a nice hot bath, and I'll bring your pajamas and make you some chamomile tea. If you don't feel any better after your bath, drinking tea, and lying down, then I'll get you some medicine.

"Now this is how you put the pad on: take the strip off the back, place the pad in your underwear, and pull 'em up tight."

"Grandma, I'm so glad you're here."

She wrapped her arms around me and I felt safe. "Honey, I'm glad I'm here too. My little Carmen is growin' up."

"Grandma, it's hard to believe that I started my period."

"Yeah, sweet pea, I know. And it was in the good Lord's timin'. Your mama told me how you near worried her to death about it. But, child, we never wanna rush God. He knows what's best for us. Not just for children but us ol' folks too."

After I bathed and drank tea, my grandma tucked me into bed nice and tight. She told me I needed to start charting when my cycle started on a calendar, so I would have a better idea of when it could possibly come again. However, she said my period might be hard to pinpoint for the next few months. She said that I should always be prepared.

When she left I closed my eyes and prayed.

Lord, I know that I shouldn't have worried about when I would start my cycle. I was not trusting You to take care of me. I'm sorry. I feel . . . well I feel a lot of things. Physically, I don't feel good, but I know that You will take care of me. Help me handle my period and do the right thing as a young lady. I love You, Lord, and these cramps aren't so bad! In Jesus' name. Amen.

✪

The next morning, I felt like I had put my foot in my mouth. Boy, was I not feeling good! Not only did I have a headache, but my stomach hurt too. I didn't think I would be able to stand up straight at all.

"Grandma!" I yelled. She came running into my room.

"Baby, what's wrong with you?"

"Grandma, my stomach hurts! It must be cramps. I don't think I can go to school."

"Let's get you some more hot tea, and you go and take a shower. I'll get you some medicine too. It's your first time, and it's going to take some gettin' used to. But you'll be okay, baby."

After lying down for a while, I felt better, and Grandma took me to school. I was an hour late because of my cramps. When I hooked up with my friends, I told the three of them that I had something *big* to tell them. They thought it had something to do with Spence.

"No. This only has to do with me."

"Like Spence doesn't have anything to do with you," Layah said.

"This is *not* about Spence," I said. "I got my cycle last night."

"You did?" Riana asked.

"Go, Carmen. It's your cycle! Go, Carmen," Imani sang, and Layah and Riana joined in.

"Shhh, y'all. I don't want the whole school knowin' my business," I said all embarrassed.

"So, how do you feel?" Riana asked me.

"Oh, this morning the cramps were awful. My grandma hooked me up, and she made tea and let me lie down. That's why I'm so late. I know y'all missed me," I said, joking.

They all giggled.

"Your mom wasn't even there? You were like Layah then," Imani said to me.

"Yeah, I guess I was." Grandmas are the best.

"Carmen, I need more details," Riana said.

"My period actually appeared brown. My mom told me it could start that way, and we learned that in health class," I said.

"Mine started off red," Layah said. "Everybody's always different, girl."

Layah replied, "Mine should be coming back any day now. Now, at least I have a friend who I can talk to about my cycle."

"Yeah, I guess that is pretty cool," I said.

✪

The following week after school, I walked in the door and my mom was there, back from vacation. We embraced, and neither one of us wanted to let go. There was no way to explain how I was feeling. I was so glad she was back to take care of me. It's funny; I wanted to hurry and grow up, but in my mom's arms, I still felt like a little girl.

"Hey, honey."

"Hi, Mom, I'm so glad you're back. Where's Dad?"

"Honey, he's meeting with a couple of his coaches."

"I can't wait to see him," I said enthusiastically.

"Well, on our vacation you had a major event occur, huh?"

"Yes, my period came and Grandma was really helpful, but I'm glad that you're here now."

"Grandma told me how you handled everything so well, and that you had some cramps, but that she took care of you."

"Yeah, she did. You know Grandma."

"Well, honey, this is another stage in your development as a young lady, and we're going to trust God with everything that concerns you. It's important that we keep an open line of communication. If you ever need to talk about anything, I've said it so many times before, but you know that I'm always here. There's nothing that's too bad or difficult for us to talk about."

"I love you, Mom."

"Love you more, honey."

"Oh, Mom, how was your trip?" I asked.

"It was spectacular, Carmen. The food was magnificent. The resort was top-notch and your dad treated me like a queen. I loved it."

I was glad that my parents had a chance to get away. They deserved it.

✪

After school the next day, my three girlfriends came up to me with a puzzling message.

"All of us have notes from the office saying not to ride the school bus because our moms are picking us up," Riana said.

"Yeah, I got the same message," I said.

"I know, it's weird," Imani said.

"Wonder what this is about? What did we do now?" Layah asked.

We all started thinking. What had we done? None of us could remember anything. Just then, I noticed my mom's car pulling into the parking lot. Imani's mom was in the passenger seat, and right behind them was Layah's grandmother riding with Riana's mom. All four of us looked at one another.

The four of *us* wondered what the four of *them* were up to.

"Hello, ladies."

"Hi. What's goin' on?" I asked.

"Get in, girls," Imani's mom said.

"Mom, why are you riding with Mrs. Browne?" Imani asked.

"We're headed to Colonial Heights for something special," Miss Bastien, Imani's mom, said.

"Why are y'all doin' this? What's goin' on?" Layah asked.

Layah's grandma, Mrs. Golf, and Riana's mom, Mrs. Anderson, told Layah and Riana to hop in the car, and they'd answer all their questions on the way to the special place.

We pulled up to an old-fashioned-looking home. As we exited the car, all of us girls were shocked. The place looked like something out of a fairy tale. We went inside and saw a table set for eight with pretty china.

We didn't have to wonder where we were going to sit. There were place cards with each of our names written in calligraphy handwriting.

"Well, ladies," my mother began, "we just wanted to let you girls know that we're proud of each of you. We're excited about your growing friendships, and we want to celebrate you growing into young ladies. So that's why we're here at this beautiful facility, where we can enjoy delicious treats and some good ol' girl talk. Older ladies to younger ladies."

I remembered my mom explaining Scripture to me from the book of Titus in the Bible, which said that older women should teach younger women.

"We moms knew that it would probably be difficult for any of you to just start the conversation off with questions or comments about your changing bodies, boys, and those things. So," Mom said, reaching into her purse, "I've brought along something to get us going."

What is she reaching for? I thought.

"This is a new game designed by my friend Miss Pam. You girls remember her from the skating rink. It's called *Moms and Daughters: Hot Topics*. The idea is for the mom and daughter to pull a card from the deck that asks questions, which they might find uncomfortable if they had to come up with the words themselves. So the cards are 'conversation starters.'"

"Oh, that's cool, Mom," I said excitedly.

Imani's mom said, "For instance, this card reads, *Will I have my cycle until I'm an ol' lady?*"

Mrs. Golf, Layah's grandma, said, "Honey, I believe I'll take that question. Grandma don't have no cycle no more and I'm sho' 'nuff happy about it. Some women have theirs well into their fifties, and some stop before. Just depends on what the Lord does."

Everybody started laughing.

Riana read a card next. "*How do I keep myself clean and fresh during my cycle?*"

"Oooh! Can I answer that?" Layah asked, surprising everybody.

"Go ahead, baby," Mrs. Golf said proudly.

"Well, I know it's important to be extra clean during your

cycle. My grandma always says that no one should be able to tell by your hygiene that you're on your period. You need to wash yourself really well, and check yourself in the bathroom often. Also, there are all sorts of special feminine sprays and powders to help ladies out."

"Very good, baby," Layah's grandma said, as all the moms seemed very impressed as well.

"I want to add something too," Imani said enthusiastically. "Even though I haven't started my cycle yet, my mom told me how important it is to always have extra pads that I can keep in my purse or locker or whatever. If my cycle comes and I don't have pads, I can check a dispenser in a public bathroom or use toilet paper to make a pad until I get some. She also told me that she and I would chart, or keep up with, my cycle on the calendar, but also to expect that it might not come at the same time each month. And that when it begins, the color could be a shade of brown or red."

"I'm impressed, Imani," Miss Bastien said, winking her eye at her.

"I want to add something," I said, smiling.

"Sometimes you might experience cramps or headaches or backaches and even moodiness. We can take pray, drink hot tea, relax, lie down, or take medicine. I've done all of those," I said, smiling.

"Good points, Carmen," my mom said.

Riana's mother, Mrs. Anderson, took a card from the deck and said, "This one reads, *I feel like boys are looking at me differently now that my body is changing. I'm starting to like boys, but I feel awkward at the same time. What's that all about?"*

Mrs. Anderson said, "It's okay to have a boy as a friend, and it's normal that as you get older, you like them a little differently than when you were younger. But remember that boys should be your brothers in Christ. Girls' and boys' bodies are developing and that's natural, the way God designed it. You shouldn't feel ashamed about it. It's natural to feel a little awkward. You have to keep in mind that your bodies are special and should be treated that way. Intimacy is for when you get married."

Mrs. Golf shouted, "That's right, y'all. No *wed,* no *bed.*"

Everybody cracked up.

My mom said, "The Bible tells you that your bodies are temples, and that you and others should respect them. You girls are young now, but that applies to you not only in middle school, but high school, college, and until you become an adult and get married."

"Mom, may I pick a card now?" I asked eagerly.

"Sure, honey, go ahead."

"What does purity really mean?"

Mom started, "Well, girls, purity is really a condition of your heart. It means that something is 'undefiled.' 'untainted,' or 'uncorrupted.' That's why it's so important to be careful of the music that you listen to, the movies you watch, even the kinds of conversations that you engage in, because your mind absorbs all of those thoughts, which later are difficult to get out of your mind. Those things take root or grow in your heart. That's why the Bible tells us in Proverbs 4:23 to guard or keep our hearts. Even the way you dress tells what's in your heart. When a young lady dresses provocative or suggestively, it says something about what's in her heart and how she sees herself. She's craving attention and doesn't know how else to get it, so she wears clothing that says, 'Hey, look at me.' Unfortunately, she'll get negative attention, which brings destruction with it. Girls, you know you see that kind of thing all the time when you're in the mall. Right?"

All of us agreed. We always saw girls in the mall dressed like they were going to a music video shoot.

My friends and I had the best time playing *Moms* and *Daughters: Hot Topics*, and the food was delicious.

Dad had given me beautiful jewelry, my cycle started, and now this special get-together; I didn't think I could take any *more surprises*.

6

Not Rich

"Clay, Carmen, Cassie, come downstairs."
I wondered what my dad wanted.

We hurried downstairs, still in our pajamas. My mom and dad were standing in the
driveway next to a car that we didn't recognize.

"Mom, Dad, whose car is that?" I asked as I
looked at the gold Lexus SUV.

My father asked, "Do you like it?"

"Yes, it's tight!" I said.

Cassie climbed inside.

"A Virginia State alumnus who owns a car
dealership has a business relationship with the
university. He supplies them with a certain
amount of vehicles."

"So you don't have to pay for this?" my
brother asked as he climbed inside and sat

on the plush leather seat.

"No. The university is pleased with what I'm doing with the football program, so this is how they rewarded me."

"Dad, what happened to our other car?" I questioned.

"Your mom and I decided to bless a young family at church who needed a car. Two of our deacons just came to pick it up. God blessed us to bless someone else."

"Wow, that was a nice thing to do!" I said.

"Mom, we have two TVs in here! Look, they're in both of the headrests. And I can see each one from the middle too," Cassie said, so excited.

"This is a three-row seater, so you can get all the way in the back," my mom said as she hopped in the car.

Dad said, "You guys go on upstairs and get dressed. We're going for a ride."

Clay and Cassie and I still had on pajamas from when my dad had called us downstairs earlier.

"Where are we going?" Clay asked.

"Just go and do like I said," Dad said, laughing.

The three of us took off upstairs to get ready. I was so excited; I couldn't believe it. We hadn't had a new car in a long time.

All three of us showered and dressed in record time.

"Now I know what to do to get you guys moving quickly—just get a new car," Dad said, laughing.

Clay and Cassie started arguing over which DVD we'd watch. I didn't care. I was in awe looking at all the neat features the car had.

"You guys know better than that," my dad said after they couldn't decide on anything. "I just told you all how we were blessed to receive this car, and we gave our car to another family. Now let's be mindful and considerate of one another."

"Yes sir," Clay and Cassie said together.

After driving for a while, we pulled into the Cracker Barrel parking lot. Cracker Barrel was one of my favorite restaurants and I was starving. I ate French toast, bacon, eggs, and grits. Clay ate his favorite: cheeseburger and french fries and a big slice of carrot cake, which he let me have a teeny-weeny piece of. Cassie ate fried chicken with mashed potatoes, corn, and a slice of apple pie with caramel on top. I was the only who ate breakfast food.

After our meal I felt so sluggish. My dad said we were too young to be so tired and that we needed to work off some of that food.

"I know just what the Browne family needs," Dad said, hitting the steering wheel, all fired up.

He said that he was taking us to the indoor track at Virginia State to work off the food.

He can't be serious.

"Dad, we're too tired to run," Cassie whined.

"That's exactly why you need to get moving, honey," My dad said, laughing.

He was the only one laughing because I didn't feel like going either, and judging from the look that my mom gave him when he made the announcement, she wasn't so sold on the idea.

Clay said, "That'll be cool because I can work out."

Of course he thought so, being an athlete with hopes of being a starter on the football team once he made it to high school.

By the time we made it to the university forty-five minutes later, we didn't feel as heavy, and we were kinda up for the challenge.

Mom was the coach, using Dad's stopwatch to time us kids. We ran around the track several times and then, just as we were finishing, to my surprise I saw Spence standing on the sidelines talking to my dad.

"Hey Spence, what are you doin' here?" I asked, walking over to where he and my parents were standing. Spence said hello to my family. Mom and Cassie left to visit one of Mom's friends who worked in the drama department. Clay went to the weight room to hang out with a couple of Dad's players.

"What's up, Carmen? I'm just hangin' out. My granddad had some work, so I just decided to come to the track and get my work out on."

"So, Mr. Spence, you're kinda diggin' Carmen Browne, huh?" Dad asked.

I thought, *He didn't just say that!*

"Daddy!"

"Daddy, what?" my dad answered.

"Spence, I know you're a good kid. You know that your grandfather and I communicate quite often. As Carmen's father, I just wanted to let you know that she and I talk a lot about what's expected of her, and your grandfather has told me what he expects from you. You know, about how she should carry herself as a young lady, and how you should be a respectful young man."

"Oh, yes sir, Mr. Browne. I'm not gonna front and pretend like I don't think Carmen is pretty. And yes, I do like her. But my grandparents don't *play* either, sir, and I would never disrespect her or any other girl. I'm not like that."

"Okay, son, just to let you all know that we're watching," Dad said, smiling, patting Spence on the back, and pinching one of my cheeks.

★

The next week in health class, we had a substitute. We could talk in small groups as long as we were quiet. So of course Layah, Imani, Riana, and myself started chatting.

Layah said, "My dad told me yesterday that your dad got a big bonus for taking his team to the championship game this season. Y'all are rich, girl!"

"Your dad got a raise?" Riana asked.

"A huge one—it was all in the paper. What, y'all don't know the 4-1-1?" Layah teased us.

"What did it say?" Imani asked.

"Carmen, do you want to tell them, or do you want me to?" Layah asked.

I was too embarrassed to look at my friend and tell her that I didn't know all the details. So I just motioned for her to speak. Hopefully, she'd enlighten me as well.

"Okay, okay," Imani said, "get to the point."

Layah continued, "The paper said the school gave him a $50,000 bonus for making it to the play-offs, plus a new car."

"Oh, Carmen, that's cool!"

"It's not a big deal."

I know about the car, but how come I don't know about the $50,000 bonus? I wondered.

"Not a big deal!" Layah exclaimed. Thankfully, the bell rang. "Oh, we'll pick this up later, Carmen."

As I stood at my locker preparing to go home, I overheard some girls saying that I thought I was so much. People were trippin' over something they'd read in the paper about my dad, and treating me negatively because of it.

★

After school my mom took me to voice lessons on Virginia State's campus. I didn't wanna say anything on the ride over. Mom was so into her gospel CD that she didn't ask me much about my day. I had to admit I was a little mad at her. She was the one who said that she and I had an open line of communication, but I didn't even know about my dad's bonus.

Okay, sweetie. As soon as you're done with class, your dad will come and pick you up," Mom said as she waved to my voice instructor.

I stood there waiting an extra second for her to tell me something big about my dad. *Shouldn't I know something?* I thought. But she said nothing.

I loved singing and my teacher said that I had a melodic voice, which needed some fine-tuning, but had lots of potential. I was practicing my scales but I wasn't concentrating. I was happy for my father. It was just that he didn't bother to share his good news with me. I was his girl! I wondered if Cassie or Clay knew. The more my mind wandered, the more out of tune I became.

My instructor, Mrs.Lopez, said, "Timing was not good. You started out great, miss lady. But now you've ended on some bad notes. Keep your mind focused and I'll see you on Thursday. Be prepared to give me a full, good hour. Comprende?" my voice teacher asked.

I didn't know how to speak a lot of Spanish but *that* I certainly understood. Next time I'd be focused from beginning to end.

✦

Later, when Dad and I made it home, I told my parents what was bothering me.

"People said that I'm rich, and I didn't even know what they were talking about." Both of my parents just started laughing. "They said that I think I'm so much."

"Sweetheart," she said, placing her hand on my head, "you're not rich."

"Girl, you don't work nowhere," my dad said.

"What about, 'what you have we all have'?" I said, repeating things they had said to me before. "So are you and Mom admitting that *you're* rich?"

I stumped my parents there for a second. I knew they wouldn't let me keep them there for long. However, I'd raised a valid point.

My father sat next to me and said, "Carmen, listen. I didn't tell you anything about the deal because it's adult business. I did really well this year. In sports there are hefty bonuses tied to performance. If a team makes it to a championship game or has a certain record, the coaching staff is given special benefits. We've exceeded several of the goals that we set for the team. But make no mistake about it; I'm not rich. There are a select few coaches who coach at Division I universities who make a million a year. We're still a small school trying to make our way. Thankfully, we're doing better financially than we have in a long time."

I nodded, understanding.

Mom added, "And I'm working now. My business is growing by leaps and bounds. It seems that I can't keep up with the demand of all the clients that I'm painting for."

My dad said, "No one's rich. We're just doing better. We're also being good stewards over the money that God has given us. That just means that we are carefully watching *how* we spend, and *what* we spend God's money on. Because in the end it belongs to Him anyway. Remember the memory verse that Mom and I assigned to you all a while back? Psalm 24:1, 'The earth is the Lord's, and the fulness thereof; the world, and they that dwell therein.' That means that everybody and everything on this earth belongs to God. They may have not *accepted* Jesus or be living for Him. But He's still in charge. And, Carmen, let me tell you what being rich is. Being a child of the Most High God, that makes you rich."

"Dad, so you're saying rich people have a lot more money, like Oprah or that Microsoft man?"

"Exactly. Even though we don't have that kind of money, we feel like we're rich people."

My mom said, "Sweetheart, your wealth comes from having all that you need in Christ. Money doesn't do that; it comes and goes. We're not trusting in our jobs. We're trusting God. That's where our strength comes from. That's where our hope is. And that's where our wealth lies. You get it, sweetie? And for those people who say that you think you're something, you *are*, honey, in God's eyes. According to the Word, you're the apple of His eye."

Hmmm. That was funny to think of being the apple of God's eye. It reminded me of a phrase that I read in one of my mom's books, *God Thinks You're Wonderful*, by Max Lucado. It said, "If God had a refrigerator your picture would be on it."

Now I understood after talking to my parents. I was wealthy in God, which was the most important thing. But in the way that people thought of Carmen Browne, I was *not rich*.

7

Truly Royal

The first day of April. That meant only one thing. April Fool's Day and everybody at school would be pulling April Fool's jokes. They couldn't get me. My guard was up.

However, when Spence came up to me and told me he was moving for sure in a week, that was one statement I hoped was a joke. I couldn't even speak. I couldn't explain why it meant so much to me that he didn't leave.

He said, "I'm just playin', Carmen. I don't know yet if I'm moving or not. It was a joke."

I nudged him softly on the arm.

"Don't do that," I said, sorta laughing.

"For real, I hope I don't move away."

"When will you know?" I asked.

"My dad and granddad are still trying to

work it all out. My granddad told me that he and my dad discussed that if I go, it would be at the end of school, so I could get a chance to transition during the summer."

Spence walked with me to the lunchroom, and he went to sit with Hunter, and I caught up with my girls.

My crew was checking out the latest happenings in the school newspaper. We chatted a bit and then headed to the bathroom. Layah and Riana were in front of Imani and me.

"Watch this," Imani said to me as she playfully touched my arm. "Ohh, Layah, don't move!"

Both Layah and Riana stopped in their tracks and turned around. I looked over at Imani, and I could tell she couldn't keep a straight face. Layah motioned for her to speak up.

Imani said, "You've had an accident."

Layah immediately hid behind Riana. "What?!"

I didn't see anything obvious, not that I was looking either. So I didn't know what Imani was referring to. Riana also had a perplexed look on her face.

When we got into the bathroom, Riana checked under the stalls to see if it was clear for us to be open. After all, we didn't want the world knowing our business. And if one of us had cycle drama then the rest of us were concerned.

"Coast is clear," Riana said as she stood straight.

"How bad is it, y'all?" Layah asked.

Imani started giggling. Riana and I both looked at her liked she'd lost it. It wasn't cool for her not to feel the seriousness of this possibly embarrassing situation. Layah looked at Imani laughing and got upset.

"Nothing is funny here, Imani," Layah shouted. "If you had a spot on your pants and still had three more periods of school to go, you'd be wiggin' out."

"You're right, and you should be glad that you don't have a spot either," Imani said as she walked up to Layah and spun her back toward Riana and me. "April Fool's to all of y'all. Got ya!"

Thankfully there was nothing on Layah's clothes. I could have kicked myself that I'd forgotten it was April Fool's Day. She'd gotten us all good.

Layah was mad though. "That was not funny."

"Ooh, come on, girl," Imani said. "Learn how to take a joke."

"You play too much, Imani," Layah said angrily, getting up in her face.

Riana and I got in between the two of them. Imani's face cringed. I knew it wasn't funny when the joke was on you, but Layah needed to take a chill pill.

Help us, Lord, I thought.

Then Layah started smiling, "Got you back, Imani. Ha ha. I'm not mad. I just got even. April Fool's."

We all hugged.

When I went home later that day, I placed a handwritten sign on my chest. It read, "*No more April Fool's jokes today!*" My family laughed at me, but I was seriously all joked out.

Later in the month, my dad promised to take me with him on a recruiting trip to Charlottesville, Virginia. It would only be a quick overnight trip, but at least I'd get to spend the night with my *first* best friend, Jillian Gray. Boy, did I miss her.

My brother and sister weren't going on the trip, so their time with Dad would be spent checking out the latest super-hero action movie. Mom and I weren't into those kinds of movies. The movie theater was in the mall, so Mom and I decided to window-shop and then meet the rest of my family later for pizza.

Though lots of things about me were changing: my body, things I liked and didn't like, and my moods, there was one thing that stayed constant. Girl time with my mom was still da bomb. Hanging with her was so much fun. She told corny jokes and she listened to whatever I wanted to chat about. Sometimes she even knew I needed to open up before I did.

As we walked down the center of the mall, I couldn't stop staring at some older girls, who were dressed really reveal-ingly. I tried not to look so hard, but I just wanted to tell them to go cover up or something. I knew that wasn't my place, but it was really bothering me. Before they saw my eyes buck wide, I turned away.

"So their outfits disturbed you, huh?" Mom asked, com-pletely feeling me.

"Yes, Mom. You wouldn't let me out like that."

"It's just what we discussed a while back during our spe-cial get-together of moms and daughters," Mom said.

My mom stopped walking and smiled at me. "Young ladies who dress revealingly may not realize the message that they're sending. Some dress that way to 'keep up' with friends who do it. Others think that it's the only way that boys will notice them. Neither of those are good reasons. It's good to know that my talks with you are having an impact. My lady-bug listens. Go, Carmen! Go, Carmen!"

My mom started doing the "cabbage patch" in the mall. I giggled, watching her dance and act silly. It was so good to have her as a mom and a friend.

"Let's treat ourselves," she said surprising me, as she checked out my half-polished nails. "You need to get these shaped up."

"You're gonna let me get my nails and toes done?" I asked, hoping I wasn't dreaming.

"Well, you've earned it. Your grades not only improved but you've maintained them. No crazy polish though, miss lady."

"Yes, ma'am," I said in a pitiful voice.

The nail salon, *Tips & Toes*, wasn't as crowded as usual.

I couldn't wait to be older. I would get to wear flashy polish, put on makeup, and get a cell phone. As I noticed my mom talking on hers to check in with my father, I imagined having one, and changing the faceplates to coordinate with my different outfits. A lot of kids in middle school had them. Maybe since she was treating me to a little pampering, she'd consider changing her mind. She'd told me two years ago that I couldn't get a phone until I was sixteen.

"Pizza Hut sounds good, Charles. We'll see you guys there at seven," my mom said to my dad. "Love you too."

She smiled as she hung it up. *Time to hit her up with the big question. She won't say no. And if she does I'll be ready with my reasons.*

91

Though I had psyched myself up, I said in a deflated tone, "Mom, I know you're gonna say no, but . . ."

"Okay, Carmen, what is it?" my mom asked as the technician pushed her cuticles back, getting them ready for a fill-in.

"Okay, maybe you'll surprise me, make my day, and say yes," I said, purposely prolonging my question.

"Girl, if you don't tell me what it is."

"It's been a long time since I've asked you this, and everyone has one." I thought, *Oops that's the last thing I should've said, because then she'd say, "I don't care what everyone else has, you're my child."* Continuing, I said, "Umm . . . if there was an emergency I'd need one, and it won't cost a lot of money and—"

Cutting me off she said, "No ma'am, you're not getting a cell phone. End of discussion."

Poking out my lips, I said, "Fine then!"

"Watch your tone, young lady. I was about to say that I'd talk to Dad, and see if we could consider moving up the time. You raised some good points and I hear you. But you know that we don't get things just because other people have them. That's what we just talked about regarding the way girls dress."

I knew I should've left that reason out.

"Who's next?" the nail technician asked.

"Carmen, you go first," my mom said. "But if you don't get that attitude in check . . ."

"I'm sorry, Mom," I said, realizing I was having too much of a pity party.

It was funny to stop myself from going too far the wrong way. I was growing up, really wanting to become a lady in a lot of ways. I wanted to wear makeup, get my nails done, have my hair really fly, and sport a cell phone. Well, I needed to act mature as well. *Plus, the Lord wants me to honor my parents. Is coping an attitude acceptable in God's sight? No!*

"Thanks for the apology. Now go soak those crusty feet."

"Mom!" I said, all embarrassed.

"Teasin' you, girl."

Moments later I eased my feet into the soapy warm water. The mixture was perfect. The massager in the water felt so soothing. Then my nail tech turned on the chair massager. This was paradise. Who needed a cell phone? At that moment I felt like a queen.

★

This was the life. For one, I had my dad all to myself as we drove to Charlottesville, Virginia. Not that I didn't like sharing him with my siblings, but when it was just the two of us, I got extra special treatment. And I was milking it for all it was worth. We'd already stopped at Dairy Queen, and that was before dinner. Yes! I could just hear Mom telling Dad that my appetite would be spoiled.

Also, I was on cloud nine because I was headed to a sleepover with my girl, Jillian. I hadn't seen her in over a year. Though we wrote a couple of letters back and forth and chatted on the phone a few times, I knew that nothing could compare to being with her in person. Looking out the window, as we passed familiar places my family used to frequent, I realized how much I missed the place. I wouldn't trade my new life for anything, but being back here still meant a lot.

"So do you still miss Charlottesville a lot?" Dad asked.

"It's weird, Dad. I sort of wish I could live in both places."

We pulled into my old subdivision and I got chill bumps. We passed my old house and all my childhood memories came rushing back. Other than the one day when I wanted to run away from home because my parents told me we were moving, I had nothing but joyful memories.

I saw a little girl riding her tricycle in my old driveway. I hoped her family was enjoying the house as much as mine had. Holding back my tears, I wondered if we really had to move. But deep down, I was very happy back in Ettrick, with new friends and everything. When the little girl waved at me, I knew she was where she should be and so was I.

Jillian barely let our car stop before she opened the door on my side.

"Jillian!" I shouted.

"Carmen Browne!" Jillian said my whole name.

Her parents were also outside to greet us. My dad exchanged small talk with them. Jillian and I cared nothing about all that. I asked my dad not to come back too soon, gave him a kiss, and then Jillian and I headed to her room to catch up.

Thankfully there were no awkward moments. Each of us

had a million questions. Neither one of us barely gave the other a chance to answer.

We asked stuff like: What's your school like? Who's your best friend? Where do you hang out? What's the latest movie that you've seen? I learned that though we were far apart, we had a lot in common. Jillian had great girlfriends, and she had started her cycle too.

We talked about school, friends, clothes, and superficial things, but there was something else I was excited to chat about.

"I want to tell you this," she said before I could say anything.

"Go ahead, but I have something else to tell you too."

She grabbed my hand. "When you left I was so sad for a long time. I was mad at the world, Carmen. I accepted Christ, and then I started learning more about God from my parents. Then in Sunday school class, we had a lesson that talked about God never leaving or forsaking us. When you went away, my mom said that God would give me some other good friends. Not to replace you, but she said because He's faithful, He won't just leave you hanging."

The tears I held back earlier flowed from my eyes. Jillian knew Christ just like I knew Him. Our hearts had been broken the day we found out that I was moving. But now we were back together sharing.

"Why are you crying?" she asked.

"Because I was gonna tell you that I gave my life to the Lord too," I said as she hugged me. "I'm crying because I'm happy to see you again, and we're still alike in a lot of ways. I feel *truly royal*."

8

Cloud Nine

"Wow! That must've been the best dream I've ever had," I said to myself as I woke up from a perfect night of slumber.

The dream was really cool. I was a princess and I lived in a big palace. I learned from a private tutor and of course I aced all of my exams. I took a field trip every day. My chef cooked whatever I wanted and nothing ever ran out. I ate fresh fruit, along with all the pizza, nachos, and candy I could eat. The best part about it was that my friends were princesses of neighboring towns too. Even though we were princesses, our parents were the kings and queens keeping us in check! There was a ball every weekend. It was nonstop fun. No one was sad.

Me being a happy princess all the time. After a while it probably would have gotten boring. There would be no challenge. Well, it was nice while it lasted.

All of a sudden, I felt a little twitch in my belly. I went to the bathroom. Just as I predicted, my cycle had started. But I was prepared and I didn't panic. I was so proud of myself. I didn't need my mom's help. I had it all under control.

As I was getting dressed for school, I could smell biscuits cooking. I couldn't wait to bite into that flaky dough. So I got movin'.

"Good morning, Mom, guess what time of the month it is for me?"

"Well, sweetie, are you okay? We charted that it should be just about this time. You act like you got it all together, but what am I missing here?" my mom said as she tried to figure out if I really was okay.

"Mom, I'm fine. It doesn't hurt that badly, I promise. And I knew it was coming. I prayed about it. I'm prepared. I can handle this today. I won't let it handle me." I smiled.

She kissed me on the cheek. "Well, that sounds awfully mature of you, Miss Carmen."

"I know. I heard a minister say it on TV. Cool line, huh? It goes back to what you said on Christmas, about not allowing your cycle to get the best of you. Remember when you snapped at me when you were trying to finish up your project?"

"Yes, honey, I do."

"Mom, I had the best dream while I was sleeping. . . ." I

just went on and on, telling her about my blissful slumber.

Then she said, " Sounds interesting, honey. Like Paradise."

"It was," I said.

She gave me a hug before she left the room and whispered in my ear, "I'm really proud of you, Carmen."

I actually was proud of me too.

✪

After school I waved at Spence's granddad, Dr. Webb, as he pulled into the school parking lot to pick Spence up. Before Spence got in the car he walked over to me.

"Guess what, Carmen?"

"What?"

"I'm not movin' after all. My grandfather said that he was glad that things were improving with my dad, but that he has to show him some stability. Like keeping a job for a while and keeping a place to live for a couple of years. So by that time, I'll be in high school."

"That's great news, Spence!" I said.

✪

Later that evening at dinner, my family ate spaghetti and a real tasty salad that I helped prepare. It had lettuce, boiled eggs, mandarin oranges, fresh tomatoes, crispy cucumbers, garlic, and chunks of guacamole, with Italian dressing. The food was da bomb.

"As we finished dinner, my dad said, "Clay and Cassie, you two can do dishes afterward. It's your time on duty.""

I smiled. It was only fair. I helped fix the meal. They had the right to clean it up.

"And, Carmen, I have something for you. My buddy from D.C. with the record label sent you this," my dad said, holding a small package in his hand.

"What's this?" I said, reaching for the package.

When I opened the package, there was a CD, with a sweet letter from the girl group, Pure Grace.

Carmen,

Hope all is well, girl. We often think of you and hope that you're enjoying our music. Since your passion inspires us so, we wanted you to check out a few of our new songs, and give us your honest opinion. Holla at your girlfriends for us.

Love,

Pure Grace

"Oh, I gotta go play this."

I dashed to my room to play the tracks.

The first two songs were really fast and fun. I was dancing all around the room, having a cool praise time. Just me and God. Remembering all He had done for me and thanking Him with every motion. The last song was called "Cloud Nine." It was soft and sweet. I went over and turned off my light. I knelt down on my knees and just listened. The basic message was: Lord, when I think about You, I'm on cloud nine.

I felt a deep connection to the songs. I felt so special that Pure Grace would think of me and send me a preview of their CD.

✪

A few days later, I woke up to a beautiful Easter morning. The birds were chirping and it was so pretty outside. I knew my family was sick and tired of hearing the CD, because I had played it over and over again.

But at breakfast Cassie asked, "Where's the CD? I want to hear the girls sing."

"Yeah," my brother said. "Go get it."

"May I, Mom?"

"Of course, honey. We'll play it in the car. That's the kind of music that we want playing in this house. Music that ministers."

We listened and sang along with Pure Grace on the way to Easter service.

"You guys ready for your Easter speeches?" she asked the three of us.

We all nodded slowly. There were butterflies tap-dancing in my stomach.

The church was packed for the Easter play. All thirty kids in our children's choir had a part to say. Most were short, but I had to close and give a personal statement of what Easter meant to me.

I'd gone over my words a couple of times with my mom,

my Sunday school teacher, and the mirror. I thought I was ready. When I stood in front of the massive congregation, I froze. My mom and dad smiled at me. Mom gave me the thumbs-up. Then I saw my dad mouth to me, "You can do it."

I began, "I had this speech all ready, and for some reason I'm real nervous, and I can't remember. It was called, 'What Easter Means to Me.' I haven't been a Christian long, but I know I feel God's love for me daily. When I'm down, I pray to Him, and He lifts me up. When I'm sad, He helps me get happy. And when I trust Him with what I should do, He guides my feet. I'm not the best girl. Over the last couple of years I've been a little mean, dishonest, not a very good friend, and the list could go on. But God gave me grace through His Son, Jesus Christ, who died on the cross for me and for you."

People in the audience started clapping at that point, but I was not finished. I knew that they were trying to encourage me. And I was happy that I forgot my speech, because I was speaking from the heart, which was so much better.

"Because Jesus died on the cross in a really painful way, I have victory." I started singing, *The Blood That Jesus Shed for Me Will Never Lose Its Power.*

After I was done singing that a cappella rendition, I got a standing ovation. But I knew the applause wasn't for me. It was because we all believed the same thing. And that was, thank You, Lord, for Easter.

✪

In school the next week, I was bombarded with girlfriend problems. None of them involved me, though. Riana, Layah, and Imani all had various little issues that were bothering them.

My response to each of them was, "Girl, I hear you. I'll pray about it and we'll talk soon."

Each of their burdens almost weighed me down worse than my heavy book bag. I decided to talk to my mom about it.

"Mom, I feel so frustrated with all of my friend's problems. They come to me for advice like I can fix them. I'm not God."

"That's a good point, sweetie, but sometimes the only Jesus people see is the Jesus in you."

"What does that mean?" I asked her anxiously, because I certainly didn't think I was good enough to ever be godlike.

"What I mean, honey, is," she said as she put her hand on my shoulder and sat me beside her, "sometimes people see that you're happy in a way that's unexplainable. Then they want you to help them get the same happiness for the things that they're going through."

"So what am I supposed to do? I'm happy because God's helping me."

"Well, that's what you have to tell them."

"How am I supposed to do that? The only time that we can talk freely is at lunch, and that's not enough time."

My mom called all their parents. We decided to invite them over for pizza on the weekend and just hang out. I

actually thought *she* could talk to my friends about God.
Who was *I* to be explaining Him to them? I hadn't known
God that long to be considered an expert.

Once everyone arrived, Mom pulled me into her studio
and said, "Listen, just speak from the heart like you did
Easter Sunday. Talk to your girlfriends. Let them know how
you really feel and why. They need to bring their issues to
God and not you. Be honest. If you need me, I'm not going
anywhere. I'll be in the studio. But trust that you can be a
witness for the Lord. Allow Him to help you. There's a Scripture that says, 'If I be lifted up, I will draw all men unto me.'
Just talk about Him; He'll do the rest."

"Okay, guys," I said later that evening. "Now we've been
here most of the day, but we haven't talked about what the
three of you mentioned to me earlier this week. You guys
have some things going on in your lives, which don't seem to
be going right. And I completely understand. But I accepted
Christ and got baptized last summer, and since that time,
things haven't been perfect, but I've learned a lot. And every
time I've had a problem, I knew who to go to. I didn't always
go to God like I should've, but I'm learning."

They started opening up and asking me particular questions about God. Surprisingly, I could answer them. I knew it
took faith to believe in God. I knew that I could talk to God
the way I talked to my friends. (I needed to be respectful, of
course). My parents said that the Bible was a road map to
help me understand God more. Also, Sunday school and
church taught me more about God.

"I want that," Riana said. "You and I go to the same church and I hear Rev. Wright preaching about God. My parents teach me about Him too, but I guess I never really thought about this whole relationship thing that you talk about. I want God in my heart."

"Yeah," Imani said. "I want to know Him too."

"How do we do it, Carmen?" Layah asked me.

"Well, you can pray and ask Him to come into your heart. And if you really believe it, He will."

We said a prayer as we tightly held hands. They each told Jesus that they believed He was God's Son, that He died for their sins, and that He was coming back one day.

When we were done I said, "I got something special to play for you guys." I grabbed Pure Grace's CD. I put it on and skipped to the last song.

As the music played, I could tell all three of them liked it. I was happy for my friends. They had the One who could fix anything in their lives. Just like the song title, the four of us were on *cloud nine*.

9

Blissful Angel

"Mom!" I rushed to my bedroom door after getting up off my knees with my three girlfriends. Mom had told me to come to her studio if I needed her, and she made her way up the stairs quickly to see what was happening.

Layah, Imani, Riana, and myself all ran up to my mom at the same time. We were so excited.

Mom sat on the bed and said, "So everyone's accepted Jesus Christ as Savior? Do you all understand what that means?"

"Yes, ma'am," Riana said. "That means we're forgiven of our sins."

Layah said, "And we won't have to go live

with the Devil. One day we'll be in Heaven for sure now."

My mom turned toward Imani. "What does it mean to you, miss lady?"

"Mrs. Browne, I feel truly happy. It's hard to explain. I hope I feel like this forever."

"Some days you'll feel better than others. However, ladies, you all have to talk with God every day just like you do with each other. Being a Christian isn't going to make life perfect, but it is the best road you can walk on. On this road you're never walking alone."

My mom was about to get up and give us more time alone, but we all sorta crowded around her even more, so she couldn't leave. She kept talking to us about Christ.

"Well, I look at it like this . . . you guys are all great friends. But a friend may let you down. You can forgive them because you know God forgave you. And when you feel alone, you don't have to stay that way. That's when you can pray to God for strength. Every answer to everything you want to know can be found with God. He'll give you clear understanding. Riana, I know you go to our church, and, ladies, you all are more than welcome to visit our church too. This is only the beginning for you guys. The Bible says that heaven rejoices over just one. Imagine what's goin' on up there, now that three new souls are in the kingdom."

We played a board game and listened to some more Pure Grace songs. I played Pure Grace's *first* CD for them too, and everybody liked it. Riana remembered when the group ministered at our church.

As I thought about the four of us, I knew we'd come a long way as buddies. And now that we all had God in our hearts, I knew we'd continue as best girlfriends.

✪

Later after my girlfriends left, I started thinking about when my family first moved to Ettrick from Charlottesville, Virginia. That made me think of my buddy Jillian. She and I had had such a good time when I spent the night with her recently. I decided to give her a call.

"Hey, Jillian," I said into the receiver.

"Carmen? Is that you, girl?"

"It's me. The one and only Carmen Browne."

I told her about how my friends had accepted Christ. We talked forever.

✪

The next day we were in the family room playing Xbox, when the phone rang. Clay and I ran to get it, and when he got there before me, he stuck his tongue out, teasing me. He was such a chump, but in a good way of course.

"Snake! What's up, partner?"

Cassie and I stayed close; both so excited to hear what was going on with our friend. We had first met Snake when we moved to Ettrick. Cassie, Clay, and myself were trying to find a shortcut home, got lost, and ran into Snake and some of his crew.

Snake started off not so friendly. But eventually he became a Christian and joined our church. He started working with my dad as an assistant trainer, and then he got a record deal singing gospel rap. Snake and Pure Grace were label mates, who recorded on the same label owned by my dad's friend. Snake and Pure Grace were even touring together. That was a concert that I couldn't wait to go to!

"Clay, let's put him on speakerphone, so that everybody can hear him and talk too."

"All right," Clay said pushing the button on the telephone.

"Snake, man, I put you on the speakerphone. Everybody wants to holla at you," Clay said.

"Cool. What's up, Browne family? Y'all holdin' it down there?" Snake asked.

"Yeah, yeah, we're good, Snake." I replied.

"So people like the record, huh?" Clay asked.

"Yep. They seem to be really feelin' it."

"Let me talk. Let me talk," Cassie urged.

"Little Miss Cassie, how ya doin'?"

"Good."

"Yeah, I hear you guys are real good. Y'all keepin' those grades up?"

"Yep," Cassie replied.

"I'm doin' my best, Snake. How's the tour? What's it like to minister the Word in rap? Are you nervous in front of all those people?" I had zillion questions.

"Okay, okay. Same old Carmen, I see! Not lettin' people answer before you ask somethin' else."

I just laughed. I was so excited I couldn't stop myself. I wanted to know a lot.

"Sorry," I said, realizing I was too hyped.

"Naw, I'm kiddin'."

"We've been prayin' for you, man," Clay said.

"And I've been feelin' the prayers. I'll be home soon. I think you guys are comin' to one of our concert dates this summer. But hold on, Carmen, somebody right here is dying to talk to you."

I took the phone off the speakerphone position so only I could hear.

"Hey, girl!" I heard Beryle say.

"Beryle!"

A member of Pure Grace was actually calling me.

"Yep, it's me. What's goin' on, girlfriend?"

I replied, "Everything's cool. Wow! What are you up to?"

"Carmen, we're just tryin' to finish recording this CD, girl. How did you like the few tracks that we sent you?"

"I loved them! And the slow tune is really nice. I sing it all the time. I even played it for my friends."

"Not too many friends, I hope. It's not even out yet," she teased.

"My three girlfriends just accepted Christ at my house, and afterwards we played your music."

"Aww, that's so sweet. Carmen, you are the best! Just a

dynamo for God. Wait till I tell Mona and Bianca that. I hear you're taking voice lessons."

"Yep. I'm doin' pretty good according to my voice teacher, Mrs. Lopez."

"Well, girlfriend, I've got to go warm up for an event that we have tonight. I'll see you soon, though. Okay?"

"Okay."

"Keep raisin' the praise."

"I like that saying, Beryle."

"It's just a little somethin' that me and my girls started sayin'."

"Get the rest of that album out soon!" I was serious about that.

"Okay, bye, Carmen."

"Bye, Beryle."

Just then the phone clicked.

"Hello," I said as I answered the other line.

"Carmen, it's Grandma, honey."

"Hi, Grandma."

"Tell your mom that I'm on my way to the hospital with Auntie Chris and Uncle Mark."

"Grandma, is Aunt Chris okay?"

"Yeah, honey. It looks like it's time for her to have that baby. So I wanted to call you all to pray for them."

I called into the kitchen for my mom.

"Mom, Grandma's on the phone."

"Hey, Mom. How are you?"

"I'm good, honey. I was just tellin' Carmen that I'm on

my way to the hospital with Chris and Mark. They think it's time now."

"Okay, call us as soon as you know something, Mom."

"I will, honey," my grandma responded.

Mom gathered us together, and we immediately began to pray for Auntie Chris and Uncle Mark. Mom asked the Lord to protect them on the way to the hospital. She prayed for smooth traffic, and that they wouldn't be nervous or panic. She asked God to strengthen Auntie Chris to ease any pain, and finally for a healthy baby to be born.

The next morning we got the great news. God heard our prayers.

Angel Gabriella was born, weighing in at a healthy 8 pounds, 8 ounces.

My dad said she was a big one.

When I finally got a chance to talk to Auntie Chris, I was so excited.

"Auntie Chris, I can't wait to see my new cousin, and I just love her name."

"Thanks, Carmen. Your little cousin is perfect and she came in God's timing," Auntie Chris said.

Boy, did I understand what she meant by that. It's best to not try and rush God. Instead of focusing so much on wanting a cycle, I should have focused on Him.

"Uncle Mark is going to send you guys some pictures over the Internet."

"Okay!" I said.

"Bye, Auntie Chris."

"Bye, sweetie."

I couldn't wait to go visit this summer and babysit. Last time I came with Cassie, and this time I knew I was coming with God. We were going to have a great time!

Later on, my family looked at Angel Gabriella's pictures and everyone said, "Awwww." My mom said all babies look alike until their features develop in later months.

Lying in bed looking up at the ceiling, I thought about all the cool people in my life. I had a good family, though my brother and sister still got on my nerves from time to time, and my parents were the best. Strict, but the best. Three girlfriends with strong personalities that I loved to pieces. For now I was just happy with the way things were.

❂

I was in my room resting after school when Cassie knocked on my door. "Carmen, you asleep?"

"No, I'm just lying down because I'm not feeling that good." My cycle was back.

"What's up, Cassie?"

"Sometimes I hear you and Mom talking about stuff, you know, girl stuff. So I asked Mama what was going on and she explained it to me."

I was a little surprised, but I said, "What did she tell you?"

"About girl's menstruation. How it comes once a month, and all that. I never ever want my period to come on! Ever!"

"Cassie, I wanted mine to come. And I've learned a lot

about my changing body since I've had my cycle."

"I'm not sure what I want, Carmen."

"Well, there's no need to rush and nothing to be scared of. It might take you a couple of months to get used to it."

"So it doesn't hurt?"

"Sometimes. Like now, my cramps are bothering me."

"Really? So it'll be okay when I get big? I'll be able to handle it?"

"Girl, with God you'll be able to take anything."

"Thanks, sis."

"If you need anything, I'm your girl. You know you can always come talk to me."

Wow, I'm sounding just like Mom. Funny how that happened, I thought.

When my sister walked out of my room, I realized that one day she'd be where I was now. She'd grow up and get her period too. I was glad we were getting closer. She was still a brat. I guess I was too. Both of us were still finding our way.

After dinner Clay asked me to play Xbox with him again. Boy, did he like that thing. And I liked the fact that I was able to beat him. But he really didn't wanna play. He wanted to tell me about Haven.

"So how did it work out?" I asked.

"It turned out cool. We're all friends. My friend George actually likes Hayli."

"The one who called himself, liking me because he thought I was older?" I asked sarcastically.

"That's him. Now he likes Hayli and she likes him."

"So is Haven your . . . girlfriend?" I joked.

"I wouldn't actually call her that." He blushed.

Whatever he was calling her, I was glad that everything had worked out.

"Oh, Carmen, guess what?"

"What, Clay?"

"Look real close. Do you see anything on my face?"

"Yeah, it looks like you're getting a moustache."

It was funny. Both Clay and I showed signs of getting older. He continued to pull on those few little hairs on his face.

Yep, my brother and I had a special bond too.

I was so glad that God had sent him to my family. I couldn't imagine him being anywhere else. What a blessing I didn't have to think about it, because all of us were satisfied with everything the way it was.

My mom had prepared a mouthwatering pot roast with potatoes, carrots, and string beans on the side. Of course, her sweet potato pie was the best! But it was nothing compared to the laughter we shared.

"What is so funny, girl?" my dad said as he walked into our family room and saw me laughing.

"Dad, everything is just so cool."

"I've got a new name for you," he said. "You're my *happy princess*. I can't call you my little girl anymore 'cause you're growing up. And Mom told me that you dreamed about being a princess. I hope I was the *king*!"

"Daddy, you were definitely the king," I said as I gave him a big hug,

✪

I couldn't believe that today was the last day of school. *Where had sixth grade gone?* I thought. I had definitely grown up a lot.

The big moment had arrived. Our teacher handed us our report cards. When I opened it and saw all *As* and *Bs*, I was so happy. I brought a *C* from last semester up to an *A*. I knew my parents would be proud. I had worked hard and was thankful God helped me to understand the material.

My classmates and I were socializing and signing yearbooks. I decided to write a short letter to God in my yearbook.

Dear God,

I know I can pray to You anytime and say anything. But I wanted to do something extra special. So while everyone is signing each other's yearbooks, I'm writing to You in mine. Thank You for this school year. This year I haven't always done my best, but You helped me to improve.

I'm thankful for my parents, my brother and sister, my friends, teachers, and my grades. Thank You for people who care about me and who are helping me to grow into the kind of Christian young lady that I should be. Sometimes, I've tried to grow up too fast, and now I realize that I need to trust Your plan for my life. My dad said that when he signs my yearbook he's going to write Jeremiah 29:11: "For I know the thoughts that I think toward you, saith the Lord, thoughts of peace, and not of evil, to give you an expected end." Thank You, God, that I don't have to worry, but that I can trust You with my life.

Love,
Carmen Browne
Your blissful angel

The author would love to hear from you.

To contact

Stephanie Perry Moore

e-mail her at
dsssmoore@aol.com

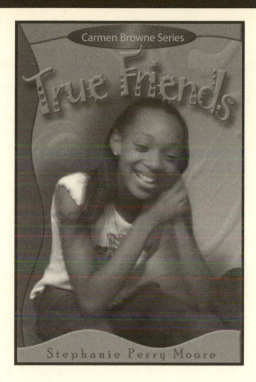

Everything is changing for ten-year-old Carmen Browne. Her dad's new job means she is in a new town, with new people, and a new school. As she enters fifth grade she's grateful for Riana, the one friend she made over the summer. But her eyesight becomes blurry, and Carmen's sense of what's important grows blurry too as she shuns Riana for a shot at popularity. Life at home gets fuzzy too when it's revealed that Carmen's older brother is adopted. It takes a school assignment about affirmative action and a timely visit from an old friend to help Carmen put life back into focus—to help her see the real deal.

True Friends
ISBN: 0-8024-8172-8
ISBN-13: 978-0-8024-8172-6

10-year old Carmen settles into her new home in Ettrick, Virginia. It's Christmas and Carmen has a problem. She's bored and her friends Rianna and Layah are bored too. Unfortunately, their boredom turns into conspiring against their parents to have a "free day" at the mall without them. This quickly turns into a lesson on honesty and how much better it is to tell the truth than to try and deceive people, especially their parents.

Sweet Honesty
ISBN: 0-8024-8168-X
ISBN-13: 978-0-8024-8168-9

They screamed by her home one Friday night and stopped in front of the Thomas's house down the street. What happened next started a chain of events that got Carmen's attention and taught her some hard lessons about domestic violence and how her own desire to be in charge can spin out of control.

Golden Spirit

ISBN: 0-8024-8169-8
ISBN-13: 978-0-8024-8169-6

Good-bye elementary school. Carmen Browne is headed to the big leagues-middle school. With a slammin' outfit, a new pink backpack, and spiral curls, Carmen is ready to face the first day of sixth grade. But knowing she looks good on the outside isn't where her joy really comes from. A full heart comes from knowing that, as a Christian, God is living inside of her.

Perfect Joy
ISBN: 0-8024-8170-1
ISBN-13: 978-0-8024-8170-2

The Negro National Anthem

Lift every voice and sing
Till earth and heaven ring,
Ring with the harmonies of Liberty;
Let our rejoicing rise
High as the listening skies,
Let it resound loud as the rolling sea.
Sing a song full of the faith that the dark past has taught us,
Sing a song full of the hope that the present has brought us,
Facing the rising sun of our new day begun
Let us march on till victory is won.

So begins the Black National Anthem, written by James Weldon Johnson in 1900. Lift Every Voice is the name of the joint imprint of The Institute for Black Family Development and Moody Publishers.

Our vision is to advance the cause of Christ through publishing African-American Christians who educate, edify, and disciple Christians in the church community through quality books written for African Americans.

Since 1988, the Institute for Black Family Development, a 501(c)(3) non-profit Christian organization, has been providing training and technical assistance for churches and Christian organizations. The Institute for Black Family Development's goal is to become a premier trainer in leadership development, management, and strategic planning for pastors, ministers, volunteers, executives, and key staff members of churches and Christian organizations. To learn more about The Institute for Black Family Development write us at:

15151 Faust
Detroit, Michigan 48223

We hope you enjoy this book from Moody Publishers. Our goal is to provide high-quality, thought-provoking books and products that connect truth to your real needs and challenges. For more information on other books and products written and produced from a biblical perspective, go to www.moodypublishers.com or write to:

Moody Publishers/LEV
820 N. LaSalle Boulevard
Chicago, IL 60610

www.moodypublishers.com